Rivals of Spring

RIVALS OF SPRING

Cliff Schimmels

VICTOR BOOKS™

A DIVISION OF SCRIPTURE PRESS PUBLICATIONS INC.
USA CANADA ENGLAND

Library of Congress Catalog Card Number: 86-60857
ISBN: 0-89693-335-0

VICTOR BOOKS
A division of SP Publications, Inc.
            Wheaton, Illinois 60187

Contents

1. A Reason To Run? 11
2. Catching a Second Wind 17
3. Shortening the Distance 22
4. The Thrill of Being Alive 26
5. Eagle on the Flagpole 31
6. The News From Wheatheart 40
7. A Boy Dragging Main Street 47
8. Running in Tune 52
9. "Last One In Buys" 59
10. "Keep Running, Osgood!" 62
11. A Right To Live 65
12. Tears in My Eyes 69
13. Afraid to Remember Out Loud 74
14. Looking Straight Ahead 78
15. A Christmas To Remember 84
16. The John Deere Place 91
17. "This Town Is Slow" 94
18. The Nicest Boy in Wheatheart 99
19. The Tumbleweed Plot 102
20. Coach Rose's Hero 106
21. Young Men's Fancies 111
22. Just Killing Time 115

23. Like Spring Wheat 118
24. Part of the Crowd.................... 122
25. The April Fool's Thing................ 125
26. The Time To Go Public................ 130
27. A New State Record.................. 134
28. "Do the Right Thing" 140
29. "I Can Run Too!" 143
30. Breakfast at the Dew Drop 146
31. The Sacrificial Lamb.................. 149
32. Discovering the Reason 154

CLIFF SCHIMMELS, like Delbert and Chuck, lived in a small town on the Oklahoma prairie. He drank cherry limeades at the drive-in, dragged Main in a pickup truck, jogged out to the cemetery, and tried to make sense out of the adult world. After college, he went back to a town like Wheatheart and taught English to the Delberts and Chucks.

Since 1974, Dr. Schimmels has been Professor of Education at Wheaton College. He is the author of several books about students and schools including *I Was a High School Drop-In*. He and his wife, Mary, have three children.

THE WHEATHEART CHRONICLES
Rivals of Spring
Summer Winds
Rites of Autumn
Winter Hunger

The smells and sounds of rural Oklahoma,
a sunset lingering in the West,
a cow grazing on the distant hill,
freshly plowed dirt, diesel smoke,
the growth and harvest of wheat—
it was all a part of my growing.
It is an inseparable part of me still.

To those people who taught me such things
as honesty, sincerity, loyalty, and the honor of work,
to those who opened their lives and invited me in,
I offer these Chronicles as a token of my gratitude.
I love you and cherish our times together
both in the present and in my remembering.

Cliff Schimmels
1985

When I became a man, I did away with childish things.

————————

1 Corinthians 13:11

1

A Reason To Run?
Fall 1981

Our story started the first day of school last fall, during second hour. I went to Mrs. Bell's room for study hall, and he showed up and sat right behind me. He spoke first, which I guess was good, because if it had been up to me I probably wouldn't have spoken for a couple of weeks. You have to realize that he was a stranger. Now, I'm not stuck up, but that's just the way we are in Wheatheart. We like folks from here better than from other places.

"Hey, we're the only guys in here." He sounded surprised. But like I told you, he was a stranger. He wouldn't know why.

"Yeah! This is a study hall for all the senior guys who don't play football." I tried to be friendly without getting myself yelled at by Mrs. Bell. This was the first time I had ever had her in study hall and I thought maybe she would be as grouchy in here as she was in regular class. Later we found out she wasn't.

I guess my answer surprised him, him being new around Wheatheart and all. "You mean we are the only two guys in the whole senior class who don't play football?" He said it like it was something really hard to believe.

Since he was already shocked, I decided to make it sound worse still. "We're probably the only guys in the whole school who don't play football, other than some of the kids who live way out."

"Football must be a big deal!" I couldn't tell whether he was still just finding out, or trying to make fun of us, in a nice sort of way, of course.

I decided to answer anyway. If I didn't tell him, he would just have to ask someone else. "Biggest thing in this town. In fact, if you ask the right people, they may tell you that it is the only thing in this town. There are some who feel that way."

"Team any good?" By now he was just asking.

I didn't mind. I like to brag about our football team even though I don't play. After all, I *am* from Wheatheart. I guess you could call this my hometown since it is the only place I've ever lived, or my dad or mom or grandaddy, for that matter. "Best around here. Coach Rose whips them in shape. We won State last year and may do it again this year. That's why everyone is out. You maybe ought to try it yourself. Ever play football?"

By then I had turned around in my desk to look at him. He looked like a football player, square built, a little stocky but not fat, and he had that football look, where you have more confidence in yourself than you probably should.

"Naw." He sounded sure of himself. "I played once when I was a kid, but I hated the game. . . . Just a bunch of big idiots running into each other."

I looked hard at him, right in his face and his eyes. He didn't laugh when he said it, and I thought I might get mad. You just can't make a statement like that in Wheatheart. Nobody makes fun of football here and gets away with it. But he had a look, it wasn't really a smile, but his eyes crinkled like maybe he meant for it to be a smile, and I figured he was just teasing. At least, I wanted him to be teasing, so I acted like he was.

But then he asked me—I knew he would. Everybody does, and I get so tired of explaining it. Most people act like they don't believe me and those who do laugh. "What about you? How come you don't play football, if it's the biggest thing in this town?"

"Can't. I'm injured." I tried to say it like I was about to die or something.

"What kind of injury?" He sounded more interested than nosy, and since by now I realized that Mrs. Bell wasn't going to yell at us, I decided to tell him.

"Ah, I got this disease."

"What disease?" He asked like he might know about it.

"Well, I've got this guy's disease in my elbow."

"What guy's disease?" He sounded as if he wanted to know, so I had to tell the whole story.

"Well, according to Doc Heimer, this guy named Osgood Something-or-other named this disease. Most guys get it in their knees, but not me. I got it in the elbow." He crinkled up his eyes again like maybe he was smiling, so I decided to tell him all about it—more than I have ever told anyone else. "Somehow your bone grows too fast and your joint turns to jelly. It hurts a lot and you're not supposed to do anything with it or get it bumped. So I had to quit football after eighth grade."

I was going to stop there, but instead, I went on. "I wasn't much good actually. I went out just because it was the thing to do here in Wheatheart." I don't know why I told him that. I had never told anyone that, I just thought it all these years—but there was something about the way he crinkled his eyes that made me run off more than usual. Or maybe, he was the only guy my age I ever met that I could say something like that to.

He crinkled his eyes again and said, "Hey, Osgood, you're all right."

I turned back around so Mrs. Bell would think I was studying, but I wasn't. I just sat there staring at my book and thinking about that remark. He called me Osgood. Nobody had ever called me anything except my real name, Delbert, except my mom who calls me Delbert Ray a lot. I just met this guy and he called me Osgood. And I told him that I don't much like football and he didn't act like he cared. Finally, when I thought I had pretended long enough, I turned back and asked him, "Where you from?"

He didn't act like he minded getting yelled at by Mrs. Bell. He talked, not loud, but he didn't whisper either. "Well, Osgood, I have lived about everywhere. My dad was in the Air Force, so we moved around a lot, all over the world, Okinawa, Germany, but the last couple of years, we've lived in California."

I wasn't surprised with that. Although I had never seen anybody from California except my aunt and uncle who came back once, he looked just like I always thought someone from California would look. He had buckskin hair and tan skin and a stocky build. Except I had never figured on that crinkle in his eyes. That one baffled me.

He went on with his story, like he wanted me to know. "My dad retired and we moved back here to be near my grandparents who live over in Alva. My dad has a little business, makes grandfather clocks in our garage."

"How do you like Wheatheart so far?" I asked. With anyone else, I would have wanted him to say something nice, but with him it didn't matter that much.

"Well, Osgood, I like it mainly because this is where I am, and I make it a point to like where I am." He didn't smirk or anything like that. "All my life I've had to listen to grown-ups gripe about where they are or what they have to do. Well, it isn't ever going to happen to me. I just won't ever grow up, if it comes to that."

I turned back around and studied that answer more than my biology book, but so as Mrs. Bell couldn't tell. It struck me as silly. Now, I had never really thought about it all that much, but it just seemed to me growing up is something you have to do, whether you want to or not.

Finally, just before the bell, he punched me in the back and whispered, "Osgood, do you ever run?" That was the strangest thing he had said so far, so I turned all the way around in my seat. With some teachers you can do that near the end of the period. If it is close to the bell, they don't want to bother yelling anymore, so they leave you alone.

"What do you mean, *run?*" I may have laughed when I asked. I can't remember.

"Run. Go out on a road somewhere and run." He acted like it wasn't any big deal.

"You mean just run for no reason at all?" I had never heard of such a thing. That is the reason God and Henry Ford invented automobiles and pickup trucks, so you don't wear out your feet. Even football players never run more than 100 yards at a time, and most loaf the last half of that.

"Hey, don't knock it if you haven't tried it." He crinkled his eyes again. "Why don't you go with me this afternoon, and we will get in a couple of miles. We may as well go—everybody else is going to be out for football."

Well, I can tell you, running a couple of miles on an August afternoon in the wheat country of western Oklahoma was about the last thing I wanted to do. What if somebody saw me? But still, I kind of wanted to be with him, and if I had to run to do it, I guessed I could run. "Okay," I said, but not cheerful. "I'll pick you up about quarter till four. Where do you live?"

"316 South Sixth Street." He was dead serious, but I had to laugh. That was the first time in my entire life that I realized the streets in Wheatheart had names, except for Main Street, of course, and the Highway. Oh, I had seen those little green signs on the corners, but I had never paid attention—never had cause to. I just knew where everyone lived. I guess he noticed that I thought it was funny. I think that must be why I decided to run with him. He could know things without my saying them.

"We bought the old Bailey house."

"Okay," I said, "I'll pick you up then."

"Where you going to tell your mother we're going?" He asked like he wanted a real answer, but I hadn't thought about that question for a long time.

In Wheatheart, sometime about the ninth grade when you started high school football, joined FFA, got something to drive of your own, and started working around, you just sort of quit asking or telling, unless of course you were going to miss a meal and didn't want your mom to do a lot of extra for nothing.

15

I hadn't thought about us being different like that until he asked the question; but I guess it does show a bit of independence, like maybe we're more grown-up than we really are inside.

But I tried not to act like I thought his question was silly. I just said, "I hadn't planned to make any big announcements, to Mom or anybody else."

He said, "Well, I have to tell my mother something or she will worry about me."

I just said under my breath—real low, "Cemetery Road."

The bell rang and we started out. But I remembered something important, or at least I thought it was important. "Hey, what's your name anyway?"

He turned and said it over his shoulder. "Charles Lavender Murphy, but you, Osgood, call me Chuck."

Catching a Second Wind

I picked him up at a quarter till four that afternoon. I drive a 1964 Chevy pickup truck. It's not really mine—it was my grandaddy's, but he died before the pickup did. Most people in Wheatheart try to manage to make those two events come out about the same. But my grandaddy didn't time things very good. He sold his farm during the depression when land was cheap and tried to buy it back after the big war when prices got high again. That's why we don't have any land ourselves and my daddy works at a co-op elevator.

When my grandaddy died, my grandmother gave me his pickup. She gave it to me instead of her other grandkids because when we were small and she made pies, I never tried to steal one.

So now the pickup is mine, but not really. Pickups aren't like cars. Once somebody else has owned them, they can never really belong to anyone else. The first owner just puts his mark on the pickup and that mark never goes away. Even yet, when people in Wheatheart see me coming, they sometimes think it's my grandaddy.

Of course, Chuck didn't. He didn't know my grandaddy. He didn't know that about pickups either, and I decided not to tell him, especially when he bragged on mine.

"Wow, Osgood," he crinkled his eyes. "Your truck even *looks* like you!"

For a starting place, we went out on the Highway to the east edge of town and parked at the Whippet Drive-In. The Whippet is one of the favorite hangouts for Wheatheart kids, especially for the football players and cheerleaders and people like that. I would try not to be there after practice when all the players were hanging around their cars drinking cherry limeades, and walking around barefoot because of blisters, and bragging about how hard the practices are. At times like that, the players need to be by themselves or at least around people who admire them. Even though I didn't dislike them, I didn't really admire them either, so I just stayed away from the Whippet after practice.

It was all right to park there this day, though, because we would be back before football was over, and besides, we could run up Cemetery Road. Cemetery Road starts at the Whippet and goes north out of town flat and straight eight miles where it comes to an end at the hills along the banks of the River. It's paved all the way to the cemetery which is three miles out, and the rest of the way it is a good gravel which doesn't get very muddy even when we get a lot of rain, which we haven't in the last couple of years.

At the Whippet, Chuck and I stripped down for some serious running. In Wheatheart it's all right to leave your clothes and everything in the pickup—you don't usually lose much around here. Most folks don't even lock their houses, and as far as I know, no one locks his car. That is just the way we are here. We do have a policeman, Earl Bresserman, who thinks he is a real crime fighter. We just let him think it, since it wouldn't do any good to hurt his feelings with the truth. I guess he does catch people for drag racing, and he takes drunks home once in a while.

For running, I stripped down to my bathing suit and put on my heaviest pair of black socks and my high-top baseball shoes. I thought I was ready until I saw Chuck. He looked like a real runner. Although he didn't wear a shirt either, he wore a real pair of shorts, good-looking shoes and gym socks, and they all had the same name,

Nike. When he pronounced that word funny, I didn't say anything. I heard once that people from California learn to read different anyway.

After all the dressing and the comparing, silent and otherwise, we got out on the road, and I almost died. Looking back now, I guess we set a pretty easy pace, but I don't remember it being easy that day. About 100 yards up the road, I ran out of breath; my side started killing me; my feet felt like they were on fire, and my legs got about as limp as a garden snake in the cucumber vines.

I thought any minute we would quit and turn around and walk back to the pickup, but we didn't. We just kept on running and Chuck kept on talking. I don't know where he got all that energy. He talked about going to school in different places and he told me how to count money in Japan and Germany. It was really interesting stuff, the kind of things you would like to know, even though you are never going to get to use it and probably nobody else will ever know you know it. But I don't remember any of it, because I thought I was going to die and it wouldn't make any difference anyhow.

But I didn't die and we got all the way out to the first mile mark. I was surprised with myself; I really was. I felt so good when we got there. This was the farthest I had ever run and probably the farthest anyone in Wheatheart had ever run. I just might have set some kind of record, for all I knew. Since nobody but Chuck had seen me do it, I didn't feel awkward about it either. With some things, it is better to do them and then tell people what you did, rather than have someone watch you. Running is that way, particularly when you are in as much agony as I was. You don't want people to see you suffer, as long as you can tell them after it is over.

But another reason I was so glad to get to the mile mark was that I thought we would walk back, but we didn't. Chuck just turned around right in the middle of the road and started running back and talking all the way. I felt like I had to follow him, even though I wasn't adding much conversation. Two or three times he said something about it being a pretty day and a nice view of Wheatheart with the elevators standing like sentries at each end of town and the high school up on the hill at the end of Main Street. I had to take his word for it—I was too busy picking my feet up and putting them down to see anything but the asphalt underneath.

I did catch my second wind a bit and manage to run a little easier for a ways. Although I didn't answer any of his questions, I at least heard them. Out of the clear blue, in one place, he asked me if I had a rope. I think I said something like, "Yeah." If I hadn't been afraid of wasting all my breath on talking instead of running, I would have told him that it was really just a long pigging string I keep around to remind me that we live on the edge of cowboy country. Sometimes I carry it in my pickup for the same reason the football players carry their old chin straps on their rearview mirrors. It doesn't really mean anything, but I guess it stands for something. Chuck wanted to borrow my rope—wanted me to bring it to school the next day. I agreed without wasting a lot of energy on wondering why.

When we got back to about 300 yards from the Whippet and I had about decided that I really was going to make it all the way back but just barely, Chuck said something like, "I'll catch you later," and he really took off running full speed. At first, I tried to keep up, but after about two steps, I went back to my jog. I watched as he held his head and body upright and kicked his heels real high behind him.

It was kind of pretty from that angle, and I almost forgot how tired I was or how bad I hurt. After he got to the pickup and disappeared around the drive-in, I jogged in trying to picture myself running like that someday. I knew it was a wild dream, but at least the idea gave me enough energy to jog all the way in, completely out of breath and aching in every muscle in my body.

Chuck was already sitting on the tailgate of the old Chevy pickup with his feet dangling down. He was sipping a jumbo cherry limeade, and he had one for me too. That was the best one I'd ever had, and for a minute there I understood why the football players come to the drive-in after practice.

After I had calmed down a bit, got my breath back, and had

enough spit in my mouth to make words, Chuck said, "You owe me two bucks."

"What for?"

"Losers buy. That's the law of the prairie." He just made that up. There isn't such a law, and even if there was he wouldn't know about it.

But I played along anyway. "That's not fair. You are going to win every day." I don't know why I said that, as if we were going to make that a daily event.

"I'm not so sure," he said, and he crinkled his eyes in such a way that I couldn't tell if he was teasing me or not.

Since I had already run farther that day than I had ever heard of anyone running, I wasn't so sure myself, so I argued about something else. "Two bucks? These things only cost 75 cents. What's the extra four bits for?"

"Tip," he said.

"Tip!" By then I had my energy back enough to act shocked. "I've never tipped anybody in my life."

He studied me a long time dangling his Nike shoes off the back of my pickup, slowly sipping a cherry limeade with the Oklahoma sun bleaching his already light brown hair. Finally, he said just as a matter of fact, "You're serious, aren't you? You haven't ever tipped anybody?"

"Nope," I said.

'You know, you're all right, Osgood. You're all right," he said, and we got back in the old pickup and went home.

Shortening the Distance

The next morning we met in second hour study hall again. Now, you may wonder why we didn't have any other classes together, with both of us being seniors and a small school and everything. But at Wheatheart we are just big enough to have a couple classes of something. And he took strange courses. While I was in FFA, he was in advanced algebra; and while I was in history, he was in singing. So we were always in different classes, except for study hall.

We talked some, but not as much as the day before. Both of us had studying to do, even though it was just the second day of school. Our teachers work that way sometimes—they give us homework almost every day, and then try to make us think it is some kind of obligation they owe us. Teachers can be funny.

Well, we had some homework and even though we're both the kind of guys who would rather talk than work, we usually do what we have to do before we do what we want to do. So we did homework. At the end of the hour, I gave him my pigging string. Actually, a pigging string is just a thin rope with a loop on one end. It is what the calf ropers use to tie a calf's feet together after they catch it and wallow it to the ground. Goat ropers use pigging strings too, but probably don't admit it since they don't even admit they rope goats. It isn't much of a sport—sort of like comparing touch football to real football.

I gave Chuck my pigging string rolled up in a paper bag so no one would see. I didn't think to ask him what he wanted it for—I just figured it was important. We made up to run at a quarter till four again and then went off to our other classes.

Actually, I was having a pretty good day.

Oh, I ached all over and had a blister on the end of my little toe. But other than that I felt good. Running two miles had made me feel great inside, like I had just won an honor or something. I know that really isn't such a big deal, but it was for me because it was the first time I had ever done it. It's like learning to tie your shoes or ride a bike or work long division. You think you are never going to be able to do it; but when you do, you find out that you are a better person than you thought you were. That's the way I felt all day, even around the football players. I don't really feel out of place with them—it's just that they spend a lot of time doing something I don't do, and that creates a distance between us. But that first day after I ran two miles, I didn't feel the distance so much.

I didn't mention how I felt to anybody except Connie Faye. She and I have been kind of special friends for a long time. My mom always teased me that Connie Faye was my girlfriend, and I guess she might have been if I didn't have this guy's disease in my elbow. I talk to her a lot, but never pester her or anything, especially during football season. I don't think any of the players ever asked her out, but I didn't want to be in the way in case somebody did.

I think Connie Faye's real pretty. She's got long hair that looks like it belongs to a girl, and her hands are real soft and tender, not like most of the women's hands around Wheatheart. Now that is my idea of pretty.

Connie Faye is the kind of person I could tell about running two miles and know she would understand. Or, at least if she didn't, she would act like she did. Well, she seemed pretty thrilled about it— talked about the wind blowing in your face and the pavement beating under your feet. Well, I didn't much remember the wind blowing in my face, but I sure remembered the pavement beating my feet.

Like I said, I was having a good day—that is, until lunch. We had just gotten out of English class. I put my books up and started around to the north hall on the way to the lunchroom when I heard the awfulest racket.

By the time I got there, a whole crowd had already gathered, including Mr. Casteel, the superintendent, who was ranting and raving and acting like his usual self. Mr. Benalli, the principal, was trying to look stern but not doing a very good job of it. And Miss McClurg, the secretary, was just gathering information so she could gossip. Since I am kind of lanky anyway, I stood on tiptoe and looked over everyone to see what the problem was. It seems that somebody had tied two doors together. In that part of the hall, the classroom doors are right across from each other and open to the inside. Somebody had tied a rope real tight from the door of Mrs. Branch's room across to the door of Mr. Harrison's room. When the bell rang to go to lunch, the people in the two rooms couldn't get out; and to make it worse, whoever did it had tied huge knots at both doors. Mr. Benalli finally took out his pocket knife and sawed through the rope. As he did, I crowded in for a closer look—and sure enough, it was my pigging string he was cutting. *My* pigging string! I almost swallowed my heart. Every big shot in school was as mad as a nest of hornets in a haybale, all because of my pigging string. All of a sudden I realized how it got there, and I remembered something Mr. Benalli once said in assembly when he was quoting Mark Twain or maybe Will Rogers—"If the desire to kill and the opportunity to kill ever came at the same time, we would all get hung."

Well, if I could have caught a certain person right then, I think I could have killed him easy enough.

You just don't do stunts like that round Wheatheart: and if you do, you don't leave somebody else's evidence around. I know I turned red—I always do, even though I have black hair.

I just turned around and went to lunch the other way. But I didn't enjoy it. And I didn't have a very good afternoon after that. Sometimes I would think I was scared; then when I wasn't scared, I was mad.

Mr. Casteel and Mr. Benalli spent the whole afternoon trying to figure out who did it. Now, where you're from, tying doors together might not sound like enough for the two big shots in the school to waste the whole afternoon trying to find out who's guilty. But at Wheatheart, we don't have too many big deals, so we sometimes make our little ones seem larger than they really are.

I guess Mr. Benalli and Mr. Casteel make a good team. Both have been here a long time. They were even here when my folks were in school and that was almost before they invented television. As I said before, Casteel rants and raves and loses his temper a lot, but Benalli just stays calm. Benalli is actually a good guy, and I think the students would tell him so if he wasn't the principal.

That afternoon they called in every junior and senior guy in school, except me and Chuck, As usual, Casteel gave them the third degree and Benalli tried to get answers. Of course, they didn't find out anything, because they were calling in the wrong people. If they had just looked at the knots tied around those door handles, they could have figured out who did it. The knots were tight and hard to untie, all right, but they weren't very pretty. Anybody from Wheatheart would have handled ropes enough to tie better knots than those, so it had to be a stranger, and we only had one. But nobody thought of him. Or me either. Sometimes maybe it does pay not to be a football player.

The Thrill of Being Alive

You might think that since I was so scared and mad all that afternoon I just wouldn't run anymore. I went once and look where it got me. By quarter till four I was still mad, all right, but I wasn't scared anymore. I think I was mad because I had been scared so long, and I like being mad better than scared.

But I still went to pick Chuck up so we could go run. That is just the kind of guy I am. If I have a problem with somebody, I don't hold it in. I go straight to that person and get it off my chest. At least, that is what I did that afternoon. Up until then, I never knew I was any kind of guy. I had never been that mad before; but since that is what I did that afternoon, that must be the kind of guy I am.

I picked him up in my old Chevy again. We drove out to the Whippet, got all stripped down and started to run just like the day before. I didn't say much, but he chattered all the time. He talked about how to say hello and good-bye in different languages; he talked about running on the beaches in California; and he would point out things he thought were pretty—like the hills up along the river, which had turned a funny looking purple because they were in their own shadow this time of day. Actually, they were sort of pretty. I don't really know what being pretty means, but I didn't

26

mind looking at them and I remember even yet what they looked like, so maybe they were pretty. I had lived there all my life and had never noticed those hills before he mentioned them.

I just kept quiet and ran with him pace by pace. About half a mile up the road, I worked the soreness out of my muscles a bit, and got to running kind of easy. Once I even caught myself breathing. I guess I had always breathed, but I had never caught myself at it until that day while I was running. I noticed that my breathing and my arms and legs were all working together to get me down the road, and I felt good. I was still mad but I felt good.

I waited till we turned around at the mile mark and started back before I said anything. By then, my legs were working easy enough that I had enough wind to talk and run both. I said about as calm as I could, "Why did you tie my rope on the doors?"

"Man, wasn't that a gas?" he said.

"No." If I hadn't been running, I might have said more. But that was really all I wanted to say. We ran a few more yards without either of us saying anything.

Finally, he said, "Well, hell, Osgood, I don't know why you're so uptight about it. I . . . "

"And that's another thing." I interrupted him right in the middle. "I don't put up with anybody cussing. If you are going to run with me, you'll have to quit that." I had never told anyone that before. Everybody in Wheatheart cussed, or at least everybody I knew did, except maybe Jimmy Charles Ericson who went to the same church with me. I never got in the habit myself, but I don't think anybody ever knew I objected until that day.

We ran for a long time without either of us talking. I figured he was thinking I was really a terrible person or something, but I had to tell him the way I felt. I don't know why—I had never told anybody else, but I had to tell him.

Finally, after what seemed like an hour of our just running step for step, he said, "Okay. You are right about the profanity. We don't need that. But that trick with the rope was a good trick, and you're wrong not to think so."

I hated to still be mad when he was trying to make amends, but I was. "Why did you do it?"

"Because I knew it wouldn't hurt anybody and because I wanted to perk up the day and because it had never been done before. I don't know why. It just seemed like fun to do. Don't you ever do anything just for fun? Do you always have to have a reason?" I think he wasn't asking just me. He was asking Wheatheart. So I answered for the whole town.

"Well, we don't go around doing things that have never been done before. Where's the fun in that?"

"So what do you do for a good time, just for the thrill of being alive?" He was still asking Wheatheart.

"Well," I started to answer right away, but I had to stop and think some more. "Somebody paints the water tower almost every Halloween, and we drag race, at least those who have fast cars. And nearly everybody plays football."

"Well, for me," he said like he was sure of it, "there's more to growing up than climbing that water tower once a year or near killing yourself in a stupid car wreck."

"You must find this a pretty boring place." I tried to sound like I was protecting us.

"Nope, Osgood. Boring is who you are, not where you are. And don't ever forget it!"

We just ran along with me thinking about that.

When I looked over at him again, his eyes were crinkled. I don't know what made me remember Casteel, but I said, "Boy, he sure was mad!"

"Yeah," he said and we both started laughing hard because we were thinking the same thing, of Casteel storming and ranting, turning red in the face and yelling at everybody. After we got through laughing, Chuck said, "I'll buy you a new rope."

I said, "I'll take a hamburger sometime instead." Then we ran side by side the rest of the way back to the Whippet, and I told him about how Casteel always gets mad and how Benalli almost never does. And I told him about Coach Rose who made football so important at Wheatheart, and how everybody loved him or at least respected him. And I told him about Jimmy Charles who was something like a friend, though he was a year younger. I might have talked too much, but I thought he ought to know because this was his town too.

At least, I thought it was his town. And yet there was something different about the way he was in Wheatheart and the way I was. I knew all about the town and the town knew all about me too. Sometimes, I didn't know whether I was thinking what I wanted to, or what the town wanted me to think. And it didn't matter that much.

For Chuck, it was different. He hadn't been in town long enough to know the place, much less think like it. And I didn't know then how he thought, because I didn't know where he came from. He reminded me a bit of Shane, a guy in a book we read in eighth grade, who rode into town from nowhere, cleaned out the bad guys, and then rode back out of town.

Here I was telling Chuck things I had never told anybody—and I didn't even know he was alive five days ago.

Since we finished side by side, we bought our own cherry limeades and drank them with our feet dangling off the tailgate again. I felt a lot better than I had the day before. I knew I wasn't a very good runner, and that we were going a slow pace; but still, running two whole miles was a lot easier than I ever believed it would be.

Right in the middle of our limeades, he got real quiet and said, "Let's do something for the football team."

"Like what?" I asked. I knew he wasn't being patriotic.

"Who's the first game with?"

"Watonga."

"What's their mascot?" His eyes crinkled.

"What?" I knew the word. I just said "What?" because I needed some time to think of an answer.

"Watonga what?" He cleared it up for me.

"Eagles."

"Good," he said. "I have an old football jersey with an eagle on it.

Let's hang it on a prominent place—just to remind the town of our foe."

"Where?" I was kind of eager, but I didn't want to sound too much.

"You tell me. You know the town better than I do."

"How about the flagpole up by the school? The janitors don't put the flag out until about nine o'clock, and nearly everybody in town looks up toward the school before that every morning, what with it being right at the end of Main Street."

"Perfect," he said. "You're a born genius, Osgood, and a real community servant too. Just think of the good we are going to do for this town."

I laughed out loud, and he just crinkled his eyes.

Eagle on the Flagpole

That night we worked like spies or bank robbers. I don't know why that was fun but it was—maybe because it was risky. I guess some things are more fun to play than to be, and being a criminal is one of them.

I don't know what would have happened if we had been caught—not all that much, I suppose—but just taking the chance was fun. I wanted to be nervous and I wanted to be scared, but Chuck was so cool that he didn't give me much of a chance. All evening long he just talked about school and places he had been and things about Wheatheart, as if this wasn't any big deal; and so I tried to act as calm as I could. Sometimes I'm not a very good actor, though.

To understand our plot, you need to know that Wheatheart just kind of grows up out of the wheat fields and red dirt of western Oklahoma. The whole town is flat except for the small hill up at the north end where the high school and football field are. Oh, there are hills in the distance most every direction you look, funny looking rocky knobs out west of town, and hills along the river about eight miles north, which curve around the east. But the town itself is mostly flat, square. Streets run east and west, and north and south. The big north and south street is Main Street which is about five blocks long. On the south end is the John Deere store with all the green and yellow machinery out front. When we drag Main in Wheatheart, we turn around in the John Deere lot. Most of the businesses in the town are on Main Street—the hardware store, the Dew Drop Inn, the two banks, Jones' Grocery where nobody goes—maybe because his cat sleeps on the meat box, and Red Bud Supermarket where everybody goes, the post office, the drugstore with Doc's office upstairs, the old picture show which isn't open anymore, the Methodist Church, the Baptist Church, and the fire station. Main Street stops when it gets to the high school. In front of the high school is a curved drive around a little park with a few bushes and the flagpole right in the middle. Of course, behind the high school, on the highest point in town, is the football field, and the eight light poles around it are the tallest things in Wheatheart, even taller than the elevators, since they are up on the hill. When you have been gone for a while and you are driving back into town and feeling good because you are almost home, you always see the elevators first in the distance. But as you get closer to town, those light poles around the football field get bigger and bigger until they take over as the most important thing in the skyline.

The main east and west street is the Highway. Of course, it has a name, Adams Avenue or something like that, but nobody knows it. In Wheatheart, we just say the Highway. All the other businesses are on it. Of course, the biggest businesses are the elevators—one at each end of town, the Co-op at the west end and the Eckhart Grain Company at the east end. The exact center of town is where Main Street and the Highway cross. Right at that corner is a big dip which during a really hard rain lets the water run down Main Street and into the gutter in front of the Dew Drop. I guess when it rains hard, that dip in the Highway has a really good purpose; but the rest of the time it just slows the traffic down so that everyone coming through Wheatheart knows when he gets into the middle of things. It just seems to make sense that we should have the two banks and the drugstore on that corner where traffic is the thickest and the slowest. Out on the west side along the Highway are some welding shops and garages. Out on the east side of town is the hospital and, of course, the Whippet Drive-In at the corner of Cemetery Road.

In all, there are 1,240 people who live in Wheatheart; at least that is what the sign out on the Highway east of town says. There is a sign out on the west side of town too, but you can't read it because someone blasted it with a shotgun. Since that happened before I was born, I don't know why the person shot it. Maybe he didn't agree with the report, or maybe the bird hunting was bad that day. You can't always understand why people do things like that.

Of course, another 1,000 people or so live on the farms outside of Wheatheart, but we don't count them except at the school and the banks where having them makes a difference. So you can see from this that we're a pretty good-sized town. We don't have any stoplights or anything—we aren't that big; but we do have a law. I mentioned him before, Earl Bresserman. Earl moved here two or three years ago when old Mr. Baker retired, and he keeps order now. Maybe order would keep itself if he wasn't around, with the way most of us feel about our town; but at least he thinks he's doing his job. He has a brand new black and white Ford which is really fast. I've heard it runs 130 miles an hour, but I don't know that for sure. In Wheatheart, people tell and retell the stories they like until they become true, no matter what they were in the beginning.

That night, Chuck and I knew that if we waited until all the old people went in from their porches, Earl Bresserman would be the only one out on the north end of Main Street. The plan was that Chuck would hide in the bushes in front of the high school until I caught Earl down at the Whippet. I would honk my horn three short blasts to let Chuck know the coast was clear, and then talk to Earl ten or fifteen minutes while Chuck ran that Eagle jersey up the flagpole. Then I'd go back and pick him up, and nobody would ever know who did it.

Well, we decided that before we jumped into such a plot, we ought to give it a trial run. For one thing, we didn't know whether Chuck could hear my horn all the way from the Whippet, even though old Chevy horns are kind of loud and do have a sound you can spot a mile off if the wind is blowing right.

Since we didn't want anybody to see us, we didn't drag Main that night. We just waited past porch-sitting time, till the town had cleared, except for some of the football players still driving around showing off their new football bruises and bragging about what they would do if they could find a girl to pick up. I don't know for sure if that is what they were talking about, but that's what they talked about every other night of the fall.

Actually, I might explain it better by telling you that we waited for the second night to come. In Wheatheart, we have three nights. First, we have the night for business when everyone is out driving around and walking around and maybe even buying at the supermarket until it closes. But after that we have the night of leisure when everything closes up and the old people go back into their houses to watch the ten o'clock news on television. That's when the young people drag Main in their cars, sit around on the hoods down in the John Deere lot, and play games with Earl Bresserman.

Then we have the night of hush when the whole town gets so quiet that you forget it has people.

Sometimes in the summer I go out and plow for some farmer until two or three o'clock in the morning and then drive back into town during the hush night. A couple of times, I've stopped my pickup and just walked up and down the middle of Main Street or even in the middle of the Highway.

It is kind of eerie—you're so alone you can do almost anything you want to do right in the middle of town.

Well, when the stores closed and the second night hit, we drove up around the school. I slowed down to almost a stop, and Chuck jumped out and hid in the bushes near the flagpole. Then I drove like I didn't want anybody to notice me down Main and out the Highway to the Whippet. When I drove through the parking lot, I blasted my horn three short blasts and then went back to pick up Chuck. When I tell it now, it sounds as if I was calm the whole time, but I wasn't. I have fairly good ears anyhow, but that night I had great ears. Any sound was about ten times louder than usual. I think I must have hit every bump in town and some which were put in just for that night. Every time I hit a bump, I heard every rattle and creak in the old Chevy. When I changed gears one time, I raced the motor so loud I was sure Earl Bresserman must have heard me wherever he was; and another time, I raked the gears so bad that I knew my dad must have heard it, even though he was home watching the news on TV. I hadn't raked the gears on a pickup since I was twelve years old and just learning to drive. But I did that night. I sure needed Chuck to calm me down. At least, with him talking to me, I wouldn't have to listen to my own heart beating all the time.

Well, I went back up Main Street, and drove around the flagpole real slow, thinking Chuck would just jump out of the bushes and into the pickup without my having to stop. He didn't, so I drove around again, this time slower yet. When he didn't come out, I stopped at the end and waited for him. I just knew Earl Bresserman was going to come by and wonder what I was doing stopped at the north end of Main Street. Now I had two problems—I had to worry about where Chuck was and I had to watch out for Earl. My heart and ears both were still doing double duty, and by now my eyes had joined them, trying to look through the dark. It seemed like I must have waited thirty mintues, but I am sure it was more like thirty seconds. It was still long enough to think through the whole situation, and the thought which kept coming back was a strange one. I kept asking myself what Chuck would do if he was in my place. I don't know why I thought that. I have never before worried about what someone else thought. But he was gone, and I just couldn't wait there any longer. We hadn't done anything yet, but I didn't want to get caught thinking about doing something. So I drove off, back down Main Street.

When I got just even with the Methodist Church, I saw a figure dart out from behind one of the evergreen trees. I slowed down a bit, and sure enough it was Chuck. He came running to the pickup as fast as he could, opened the door before I could even stop, jumped in and slammed the door. He was so out of breath he couldn't talk.

After he had panted three or four times big, he said, "A beast."

"What?" I guess I heard what he said, but since it didn't make any sense, I had to ask.

"I just got chased by a beast." He was still panting.

By now I had visions of elephants or lions or an ape out of a Tarzan movie. I know that sounds farfetched, but on this night, I forgot I was in Wheatheart. "What kind of beast?"

"Big furry thing. Came up behind me when I was in the bushes up by the flagpole."

By now, I was beginning to get a little clearer picture. "A dog?"

"Huge furry dog. Looked more like a bear."

By now, the picture was completely clear, and I started laughing. I know it wasn't the right thing to do with him so scared, but I couldn't help it. I might have laughed because it was really funny, or because I just didn't want to be scared myself; but for a long time we drove down Main Street with him glaring and me laughing. When I got enough control of myself to make sense, I said, "That's Doc's dog, Spencer."

"Who?" He was still scared and a little mad.

"Doc Heimer. He lives right around the corner, and that is his old dog. Half collie. Half German shepherd. Town pet. Lies outside the drugstore in the shade all day." I started laughing again. I just couldn't help it. The picture was too funny. Here we were, plotting some deal like we were master criminals, and the brains of the outfit was being chased all over by the town pet.

Finally, I said, more serious than joking, "I thought you weren't afraid of anything."

"I'm not," he was calm again, "just dogs—and typhoons."

We looked at each other and he crinkled his eyes. I liked him more than I ever had before.

By then I thought of our big question. "Did you hear the horn honk?"

"Nope," he said, "I didn't hear anything except my feet hitting the street and that beast breathing down my back." This time we both laughed.

By the time we finished laughing and built our confidence back up, and I had convinced Chuck that old Spencer probably didn't even have teeth anymore, the night was between leisure and hush, a time when the stars are a little brighter, and the air is a little stiller, so we decided to go on with our plan even though we hadn't tested the horn. There is something in the air about that time of night which tells you that all your plans will eventually work out anyway, so you get bold enough to try almost anything. We had already laughed ourselves past silliness, and we were going to act out our plan before we lost the hush of the night or our cònfidence.

And the plan purred perfectly. I drove up around the flagpole park, Chuck jumped out and hid in the bushes, then I drove right on down to the Whippet, and caught Earl Bresserman just ordering his evening chocolate milkshake. As I drove up, I honked three times and waved at Earl so he would think I was just being friendly. He looked around, waved back like he was glad to see me, or at least was glad to be seen by me. I ordered a cherry limeade, and then he and I leaned across the hood of his new black and white Ford and drank and talked. We really don't have that much in common, but with Earl you really don't have to have much in common to talk. He likes being himself, and he likes being the cop, and he likes talking about it, especially to kids, because he wants to be our friend and the law at the same time. So we talked about how fast his car was, and he told me about big arrests he made when he was a cop in some big town out east. He talked like he wanted me to envy him a bit, but I didn't. That night I had already had about as much excitement as I could stand, and even if Earl's life was as exciting as he told it, I didn't envy him at all. I was glad he liked to talk though, because I wouldn't have been much good in the conversation. It was all I could do to keep my thoughts sorted out, with thinking about Chuck and the flagpole rope and Doc's dog and trying to catch enough of what Earl was saying to answer, "Yes, Sir," and "Well, I declare," once in a while. But I managed, and we got through the conversation and I watched Earl drive west on the Highway past Main Street. Then I went back up to the high school and around the flagpole park. I slowed down, Chuck ran out of the bushes, jumped into the pickup, held up his thumb, crinkled his eyes, and said, "Perfect." We laughed again, but it wasn't like the time before. This time it was the kind of laugh you laugh when you have done the job you didn't think you could do. I drove down the hill a bit and looked in the rearview mirror to see our accomplishment. It was there all right, hanging right on top of the flagpole, dim but readable in the moonlight—a white football jersey with red letters which announced for all to see, *Eagles 22*.

To make the plot even better, we didn't turn around to inspect what we had done, but just drove straight home. I slept fairly well, considering the kind of night I had had. The next morning I took a different route to school—I went down Main Street and made a U-turn at the John Deere store. Then I looked up toward the high school and the flagpole. The jersey was still there. Although I couldn't really make it out until I got almost up to the drugstore, I still knew that it wasn't the flag. That meant everybody in town who looked up toward the high school that morning would know something was out of place, and in Wheatheart, that in itself is big news.

As I drove closer, and the jersey and the letters became really clear in the sunlight, I tried to remember the night before, but it was sort of hazy and unreal, like something I had read in a book or imagined.

Since I usually get to school just before the bell rings, I didn't hear whether anyone was talking about it or not.

In second hour, Chuck and I swapped "Hi's" and kept our faces straight even though we were laughing inside. Luckily, we both had some work to do, so we got busy and didn't have to look at each other. About halfway through the period, Mr. Benalli's voice came over the intercom. He was calm and clear, like he always is.

"May I have your attention for an announcement please. I am sorry for the interruption. . . ."

At that point, Casteel burst in and he wasn't calm. "As all of you know by now, our campus was vandalized last night. Vandalized.

Some hooligans from Watonga obviously ran one of their old football jerseys up our flagpole. You saw it. It was there when you came to school. Now, I know that if you have any school pride at all, you are burning mad like I am. There is no excuse for this kind of behavior. I also know the thing you want to do is to retaliate—to go to Watonga and try to get even. But that isn't the way we work at Wheatheart. No siree. We don't work that way at all. We get even-" and he paused like he really wanted us to hear—"on the football field. And that is what we are going to do. Come a week from Friday night, we will just show those Watonga people that they can't do such a thing to our school. And you can bet your bottom dollar on that too."

I turned around and looked at Chuck. Right then, I wished I knew how to crinkle my eyes so people wouldn't know whether I was laughing or just easy. He only said, "You're all right, Osgood. Let's run again tonight." And we both went back to our homework.

The News From Wheatheart

That afternoon I found out what running is good for. If you go far enough out in the country, you can laugh and no one will ever know what you are laughing about. Both of us needed to laugh, particularly after Mr. Casteel's announcement, and as soon as we got past the Whippet, we broke loose. Well, at least I laughed hard, and Chuck mostly crinkled his eyes.

I don't know whether it was funnier for me because I know Casteel pretty well or funnier for Chuck because he didn't know him, but it was still funny. We hadn't hurt anybody and it only took about three minutes to correct everything we had done. But it was still funny mainly because Casteel had taken it so seriously.

After I had settled down from laughing so hard that I didn't have tears in my eyes anymore, Chuck asked, "How is the rest of the town taking it?"

"Oh, it's big." I said that like I was one of those newsmen on television who always know so much about what is happening in the world.

Then I had to hedge a little. "Well, I really haven't heard anything yet because I have been in school all day, but it's big news. And you can bet your bottom dollar on that too." I mocked Mr. Casteel when I said the last part and then started laughing again.

"Do you think everybody in town is that mad?"

"Naw." I assured him. "Just Casteel and maybe some of the real old-timers who have already forgotten how they were when they were growing up here."

"So what do people in town think of Casteel and the way he acts about things?" He was asking questions I had never answered before, had never even thought about before; and they were kind of tough, even if this is my hometown.

"I guess they just believe him because he is supposed to be smart about things; but they act like they wish he wasn't."

"Why is he like that?" He asked another tough question.

I thought of my answer quickly, but then I wasn't sure it was right until I thought about it some more. Finally I said, "Well, he has to act that way. After all, he's in charge of things, and he has to let people know it. He can't go through life laughing at kids' pranks. He has to take things serious. That's what it means to be grown-up."

When I got through, I was kind of happy with my answer until he asked, "Why?"

"Well," I said, "because adults are in charge of things. Kids like us—we just have to think about ourselves but grown-ups have to think about other people too, so they can't always laugh at what's funny."

"So that's what it means to be grown-up?" He asked like maybe he was really trying to find out.

That gave me a good feeling so I said, "Yep. That's what it means. When you have to worry about more people than yourself."

I guess my answer must have satisfied him because we ran along and didn't say anything for awhile. Then he said, "Hey, maybe this will get into the paper, a picture or an editorial even."

He said it like he didn't care whether it was so or not, but was just wondering, so I set him straight. "Nope."

"Why not?" He wasn't mad or anything, just asking. "I know there is a paper. I saw the office across the street from the Dew

Drop. *The Wheatheart Chronicle* and Printing Supplies."

"Yeah, we have a paper. Comes out every Thursday. But this isn't the kind of thing old Mr. Reilly prints." I reported like I was an expert.

"Why not? It's news. You said so yourself."

"It's not what Mr. Reilly thinks is news." I told him the best I could, but it was kind of hard explaining it to someone not from Wheatheart.

"I don't understand." He said exactly what I thought he would say. "News is news, isn't it?"

"Not when you own the newspaper," I told him. "News is what you think it is."

"So what does Mr. Reilly think is news?" By now he wasn't just asking. He was beginning to sound like he was in a hurry to get somewhere.

"Well, he is really proud of the legal notices." I reported.

"So what are legal notices?" He acted like he didn't even care that he didn't know about legal notices.

"That's when they print this stuff in small print when somebody dies and leaves his stuff to his kids, or a farmer sells his land, or something like that. It is really important stuff, written in lawyer talk."

"Does anybody read them?" he asked. It was the first time I had ever thought about it. I didn't know anybody was supposed to read them.

"Maybe the lawyers do, and maybe the people who are supposed to inherit the stuff."

"So why do people buy the paper?"

"We also have the Busybodies." I used the word before I thought. He wouldn't know about that, because Busybodies is our special word for part of the paper.

He asked anyway. "What are the Busybodies?"

"Those are the little stories all through the paper that tell us who had Sunday dinner where and whose aunt is visiting from California. That's really the newsy part of the paper."

"That's not news," he said, like he was my teacher or something. "So what do you think news is?"

"Well, important things like hurricanes and earthquakes and terrorist activities and summit talks." He still sounded like a teacher.

"I don't think so." It was my time to sound like a teacher. "You don't even know those people."

He just said, "You're all right, Osgood," and he sounded like he had his eyes crinkled. "But if the flagpole isn't news in the paper, where is it news?" He was trying to find out about the town again.

"Probably at the John Deere place." I knew when I said that I would have to explain, but that was all right. If he was going to live in Wheatheart, he needed to know. "You see, these guys meet at the John Deere place every day and talk about what's really happening around town."

"What guys?" He asked like this was all new to him.

"Well, every time the farmers come to town, they always stop in at the John Deere place and then a lot of the other men around just go by every day for a few minutes to find out what's happening and what people think about it. Even my dad stops in every day at his lunch hour just to see who's in town and what's happening."

"Sounds like a gossip party for men." He sounded like he wasn't much interested.

"Well, it isn't. It is actually pretty important. Since the paper only comes out once a week, it wouldn't do much good if it did print the news. It would all be pretty old by Thursday. But at the John Deere place, you can stay up on things every day. And you don't just find out what's happening—you find out what people think about it too." When I finished, I was glad I had the chance to tell him about the John Deere place. If someone else had told him, he might not have understood it as much.

Finally he said, "Well, if that's the case, maybe we should check out the John Deere store and get the community commentary about the new flag."

Although I wasn't sure I knew what a community commentary was, I was pleased that he wanted to go and also pleased that I had the chance to show him another part of town, and a valuable part at that. I said, "Sure, this is a good time to get you acquainted. Besides, maybe you can tell your daddy and he can get into the habit of going down every day, just like the other men in town."

"I don't think so," Chuck said. "My dad is only interested in things like hurricanes and earthquakes and summit talks."

When we got back to the Whippet, we drank our limeades and slipped back into our clothes so no one would know we had been out running. We also decided that we would buy an oil filter for the old Chevy so we would at least have an excuse for going to the John Deere place. Even though my dad goes every day, and I know everybody there, I still feel better if I have something to buy. It just makes me fit in a little quicker than going in and standing around. And that day we didn't want anybody to get suspicious.

When we got there, I saw a bigger crowd than usual; and something in the air made it seem very important. Of course, Chuck wouldn't have known the difference, but I felt it and I got really scared that maybe they were all as mad as Casteel about the jersey on the flagpole. If we hadn't already been in the front door, I might have turned around and left. I'm not very good at acting like I don't know about something when I really do.

But we were already in, so we almost had to stay. Mr. Garland, Scotty's dad, was sitting in his office. Well, it really isn't an office—just three plastic partitions around his desk, where he takes customers when they buy something and want to talk private. I am not sure I know why all that is necessary, because when anybody buys something like a tractor or a combine, the news gets all over town in about ten minutes anyhow, and not just who bought it but how much he paid and how much he got for his old one. I have never figured out why they want to talk private in the first place, but that is why he has an office. Today, he was sitting in it but he wasn't private. He was the center of attention. Everybody was crowded around him talking excited and listening close, and Mr. Garland looked like he was glad he wasn't private.

It would save a lot of time if I could say it was the usual crowd, but that just wasn't true. Sure, there was always a crowd and the crowd was always talking about things like wheat prices and football, and if you didn't know what you were looking for, you might think the crowd was always usual—a few farmers, a few retired farmers who hung around now that they had the time, plus whatever Garlands happened to be in town. But all those people who made up the crowd were different, and when you stop to think about each one by himself, you realize that there is no such thing as a usual crowd. No. There is always a crowd and that crowd is always talking, reporting news, commenting on the news or just telling stories, but the crowd is never usual.

That afternoon they sure weren't usual because they were excited, and they gathered around Mr. Garland all trying to get into the conversation. Chuck and I just stood on the outskirts and listened for a few minutes. Something had stirred them up and we were afraid we knew what it was.

"Well, Scott, you told it like it is." Someone was saying.

"Worst I've ever seen," another answered.

"I'll tell you. I just don't know what it's coming to."

"Gets worse every year too. Just don't get no better."

"It's time somebody told them."

"Maybe those guys in Washington will hear it and do something."

"If there is still time left."

"Got to be time. Just be too bad for this country if they don't do something."

By then, I was halfway between being really scared and confused. All we did was put an old jersey on the flagpole. I didn't think that was worth telling Washington about, but what else could get them so upset in their talk. Oh, they always griped about not enough rain, or about Washington controls or about the way the school ran or about long-haired hippies. But today they were so serious.

About then Mr. Garland walked around the corner of the partition and taped something to it. It was a clipping from a magazine, *Time* magazine in fact, so Chuck and I stepped a little closer to read it. The headline said, "Things Are Down on the Farm," and about halfway down some of it was underlined so I read that. It was written to sound official.

> According to Scott Garland, implement dealer in the wheat country near Alva, Oklahoma, the wheat yield last summer was one of the highest in recent history; but the price of grain, contrasted with the price of production, yielded less operating margin than any time since World War II.
>
> Garland said, "People who don't understand things are blaming the farmers for getting themselves into debt in the first place, but they have to have equipment and fertilizer and seed and Deisel if they are going to grow anything. That record yield proves they are working hard.
>
> "So they go broke and can't plant next year. What happens to this country's standard of living then?"

I read it over again just to make sure I was really seeing it. There it was, someone I actually knew was quoted in *Time* magazine for the whole world to see. Now I don't want you to think that Mr. Garland and I are the best of buddies, but I know him and he knows me and he has actually been quoted in *Time*. That is exciting.

But when I read it over the second time, I saw something I missed at first. It said, "In the wheat country near Alva, Oklahoma." He didn't say he was from Wheatheart. I don't know why, but I just blurted it out, "It doesn't say you are from Wheatheart." I shouldn't have said that. Someone else was even talking at the time.

Mr. Garland just said under his breath to me, so as he wouldn't interrupt the other guy talking, "It's too hard to explain where Wheatheart is when you talk to people on the phone."

Chuck and I backed out of the tight circle, stood on the outside just long enough to realize no one had time for the flagpole news, and then went home. But I still didn't know why Mr. Garland wouldn't say he was from Wheatheart.

A Boy *Dragging* Main Street

That night after supper I was still thinking about the *Time* article and Mr. Garland, so I went in to help my mom with the dishes. That isn't really something I do all the time. I think my mom likes it when I do, but she would never ask me to. But it does give us a chance to talk. Washing dishes is good for that. You work side by side and you aren't going anywhere. You have to pay attention to what you're doing but not too much, so you may as well get caught up on your talking.

I don't know whether my mom is smart or not, but I learn a lot talking to her. She used to be smart. In fact, she was valedictorian of her class at Wheatheart. Think of it—the smartest one in the class. I'll never make that, for sure. I know she was valedictorian because she talks about it some, but then she married my dad and had me and my little sister. Now she stays home mostly and makes a lot of things for the house, crocheting and crafts and drapes and things. I know there is more to the story than that, but I don't know it all. Parents are funny—they are always telling you little stories thinking they are telling you their whole life's story, but they always leave gaps so you never know where it all fits. Maybe they ought to pass a law which says that parents should sit down with their kids and tell them the whole life story just once, from front to back, so the kids would know where those little stories fit.

But that probably wouldn't work either because then the kids might get to know their parents too much and lose respect for them. Sometimes the more you know about a person, the more you respect that person, but it doesn't always work that way.

Even though I have to fill in some gaps in the story, I still like talking to my mom. For one thing, she never stops what she's doing to talk. She just keeps working, and that way I don't feel I'm bothering her when I ask dumb questions. That night, for example, I knew what I wanted to say, but I didn't quite know how to say it, so I beat around the bush a bit. It didn't matter. We were still getting the dishes done.

Of course, I was wiping and putting away. When two people do dishes, the one in charge washes and the other wipes and puts away. Somehow washing requires more responsibility than wiping and putting away, but I'm not sure how.

After I had bragged about supper and griped about school and had taken care of all the things you can talk about without thinking, I said, "Mom, have you ever wished you live somehwere other than Wheatheart?"

"What kind of question is that, Delbert Ray? Are you the one who's been putting those Tupperware bowls inside each other?" She kept working and being a mother at the same time.

"Sure, what's wrong with that? Where do you think you would like to live if you didn't live in Wheatheart?" I asked the second question quick.

"I never said I wanted to live anywhere else. If you put those bowls in the cabinet that way, I have to look through everyone to get the one I want. Keep them separated."

"Yes, Ma'am." I don't have to say "Ma'am" to my mother anymore if I don't want to. At least I don't think I have to. I have never tried it any other way to know for sure and I don't think I ever will. I just like saying "Ma'am"

"Why have you never wanted to live anywhere else."

"Because you don't think about such things." She answered like I shouldn't have asked such a dumb question.

"You must have thought about it." I teased her a bit. "Sometimes when you were down in the cellar during a tornado alert or when you were locked in the house during a really bad dust storm, or when it didn't rain enough to make your garden grow, haven't you ever thought that you would really rather live somewhere else?"

"Delbert Ray, you ought to know by now that no place is perfect. Florida has hurricanes and California has earthquakes. Put the big cups in the back and the small cups in the front."

"Why?" I don't know whether I was teasing still or really wanted to know.

"Because that's the way you organize a kitchen, Silly." She began to smile a bit with all my questions.

"Says who?" I smiled back but I still asked.

"Nobody says so. You just do it that way." She went back to paying more attention to her washing than to my questions, but she was still smiling.

But I wasn't through teasing. "But what if you just once didn't put them that way. What if just once you put the little ones in the back and the big ones up front? Who would tell? Who would ever know?"

"I declare, I don't know where you get all that silliness. No one would ever know. This is the way to organize a kitchen and I organize my kitchen that way because I want to. I don't need anybody tattling on me to make me do things right. Wipe that silverware one piece at a time. Don't just hit it with a lick and promise and throw everything in the drawer like that." She was still smiling, but she was serious.

"Why?" I teased again, "Is this another one of those rules that somebody nobody knows thought up?"

"Well, I don't know about you, but I know I don't want to eat from spoons that haven't been wiped dry. Why are you arguing so much tonight?" She looked at me like she does just before she takes my temperature.

Now it was my time to smile, for protection if for nothing else. "Oh, I got a lot of things on my mind." I tried to make that sound like I was forty years old and important.

"Sure," she said, "I know you do, Dear, and I appreciate your taking time out to help me with the dishes."

Although I couldn't tell whether she was just teasing or really cared, I wanted her to really care, so I asked some more questions. "When did you just decide that you would live in Wheatheart all your life?"

She slowed down in her washing a bit as if she might be thinking too. "I don't think you decide that you will live in Wheatheart. You just do. I remember a movie I saw in high school called *State Fair*. Pat Boone said to this city girl, Ann Margaret, I think it was, 'You don't decide to be a farmer. One day you are a boy feeding chickens and the next day you are an old man feeding chickens.' Well, that was the way it was for me. One day, I was a little girl playing house in Wheatheart and the next day I was a grown woman playing house. That's just the way things are."

"But it didn't have to be." I don't know why I protested. She didn't sound sad about it or anything. "You are smart. You were valedictorian of your class. You could have been a lot of things, done a lot of things, gone a lot of places."

"That's silly too. I am doing exactly what I want to do." She smiled at me like I should understand.

"Like what?" I don't know why I said that like I didn't believe her.

"Being your mother." By now she was on pots and pans so she gave the bean pot more attention than it really deserved.

"Okay, you're a good mom." When I said that she concentrated on the bean pot even more. "But isn't that kind of a big sacrifice, to spend all your time and smarts on Alice and me? Wouldn't you really like to have something for yourself?"

She moved over and started cleaning the stove. "It is no sacrifice at all. I don't even know what that word means. I am your mother. That's what I want out of life—that and maybe an automatic dishwasher." She did more than smile. She giggled a bit.

I was glad she did, because I needed to laugh just then, so I did. Then I got serious again. "Mom, Mr. Garland got his name in *Time* magazine."

"I know." She sounded like she was happy we were on a different subject. "I saw it on the bulletin board at the Red Bud." I don't know whether this happens in big towns or not, but in Wheatheart our big grocery store has a bulletin board where people put up important notices like things to sell or buy, and wedding announcements.

"What did you think?" I tried to sound like I hadn't formed an opinion yet.

"Well, I was proud of him for getting in such an important magazine and I was proud of him for what he said about the farmers. It's about time this country finds out the way it is for people who make a living off the farms."

I let that soak in a bit and tried to understand it, but there was something still more important on my mind. "What did you think about it not saying he was from Wheatheart?"

"Oh, I didn't notice. When you finish wiping, hang that towel on the back porch so it will be dry by morning, will you, Dear?" Since she had finished, she went into the living room to help my dad watch television.

I finished wiping, hung the towel on the back porch, went out, got into the old pickup and dragged Main Street from the John Deere place to the high school for about thirty minutes. I waved at everybody and yelled out the window a couple of times, but I didn't stop and pick anybody up. I just sat in the cab alone and remembered that I was just a boy dragging Main Street of Wheatheart.

Running in Tune

Even though we weren't in the news, Chuck and I ran the next afternoon, and every afternoon all fall, except on Sundays when I couldn't run. Although I couldn't tell if we were getting faster, I knew it was getting easier. In fact, two miles got where it wasn't much exercise at all. I couldn't tell anybody that, because in Wheatheart nobody understands doing anything unless it has a reason to it, and as best as I could tell, there wasn't any real reason why we were running. We just liked doing it.

We talked a lot and got to know each other really well, both through the things we said and even through the things we didn't say. Sometimes we would run along and chatter like a couple of prairie dogs on a warm morning. Although Chuck never told me about any of his friends or anything personal before he got to Wheatheart, he did tell me a whole lot about the other places he had lived and seen. And I listened and remembered what he said, a lot better than I had in seventh grade when we read some of the same stuff in that old orange geography book. When I read it back then, I really didn't pay much attention because I just thought somebody had made it up to put it into books. But when Chuck told me, I knew that real people lived that way, and it became important.

In turn, I told Chuck everything about Wheatheart. Wheatheart is a pretty interesting town, particularly if you're going to live there; and sometimes I even made it more interesting than it actually is. I caught him up on the history of the town all the way back to the land run of '89. Although I never knew anybody who knew anybody who had made the run, I told it like I had been there. Since my dad remembers when the elevators were built, I told him about that, and how the adults gather either at the Garland's John Deere store or the Dew Drop and talk about everything in town, but mostly about wheat prices and football.

I told him about Jimmy Charles Ericson. Although Jimmy Charles was a year younger, I had always liked him more than about anybody else, so I guess that made us friends. We didn't talk that much, but we thought a lot alike. He worked hard out on his dad's farm, and he played football—center—but sometimes he acted like he didn't enjoy it that much.

I told Chuck all about Jimmy Charles, thinking he would tell me about his old friends. But he never did.

Sometimes, we wouldn't talk at all. We would just run along step for step, breathing and running in tune. Even though we didn't talk during those times, running was easier because we were with each other. Sometimes, when we would get to running in tune like that, he would interrupt the silence to point out something he saw or heard or smelled.

"Wow, look at that hawk chasing that rabbit over on that field."

"Smell that odor. Is that thistle blossoms?"

"Notice how the dirt smells different now that the farmers have plowed."

"I've never seen heat rays bounce so high like they do off the elevator roof."

"Listen to that. Is that a bobwhite quail calling its babies?"

"Even the evergreens up on the hills look like they are turning colors this time of year."

It's funny that he noticed those things, because I never had. I had lived there all my life and had never really paid attention to any of that until he made me. Then it was fun to notice and even to remember it later in the evening.

But there was one thing we never talked about—why I couldn't run on Sundays. I wanted to tell him, particularly during those times when he was pointing out the hawks and the smells, but I just couldn't bring myself to it. This is the most important thing in my life, and maybe that is why I couldn't talk about it. It seemed too personal and made me feel too good to explain to anybody else. I think he might have understood, but I just couldn't tell him. I didn't run on Sundays because of my church. It isn't like we are a bunch of religious nuts or anything. I am the only one in my family who even goes. I started about three years ago when my Grandma first gave me the old Chevy. I wanted to drive somewhere so I drove up to the Baptist Church, and I have been going ever since. There is something real to this business of being a Christian. Some rules like school rules and work rules you follow because you have to, even if they don't make any sense. But with Christ it's different. You follow His rules because you want to. I didn't run on Sunday because of His rule. I wouldn't have got into trouble with anybody, not even with Brother Bob the preacher, if I had broken the rule, but I just didn't feel like it. So I didn't run on Sunday. When Chuck asked me, I just said, "I can't run on Sunday—because of my church." I didn't say any more, even though I know I should have.

He just said, "That's okay. We probably ought to rest one day a week anyway. It will be better for our bodies." I don't think he understood anything about Christ's rules, but sometimes he sounded like it.

But we did more that fall than just run together. Chuck came over to my house a lot. I never went to his house, at least I never went inside. I did meet his mother and father out in the yard once when I went over to pick him up. He introduced us just like we had been taught to do it in English class. He said, "Delbert," that is the first time he ever called me anything except Osgood. I didn't know he knew my real name. "Delbert, this is my father and mother, Mr. and Mrs. Murphy." That was it. We shook hands and everything, and everybody said, "Nice to meet you." But it wasn't too friendly. At my house, everything was different. One day while we were running, Chuck asked me about the cheeseburgers at the Dew Drop.

"They are all right, I guess," I said. "Why do you want to know?"

"Oh, I've got to eat out tonight and I don't much want to eat at the Whippet." He didn't explain why but I understood. The football players would still be there after practice. Even though he seemed to get along with them all right, that was the wrong time to be around them.

"Why do you have to eat out?" I wasn't really nosy, but we were just talking and it seemed appropriate to ask.

"My folks have gone to Alva for the night." That's all he said.

I didn't ask anymore. Sometimes you can just tell when people don't want to talk about something, and this seemed to be one of those times for him. Even though he never said anything bad about his folks, I could tell that he wasn't as close to them as he wanted to be.

"Why don't you come home and eat with us?" I asked. I know that might sound strange to some people, but at our house it would be all right. My mom doesn't get much scared of emergencies, and besides, I had talked about Chuck at home enough that she was probably hoping I would bring him home with me. She does a good job in the house, and likes the chance to show it off. She also liked the fact that I had a friend.

Well, Chuck came, barged in the house behind me, walked up first to my mom and said, "Hi. I'm Chuck." Then he did the same thing with my dad, and then from then on, both folks acted like he was my brother or something. And he acted like it too, except he was politer. That night, and when he came over other times, he bragged on my mom's cooking a lot, particularly when she cooked Wheatheart things like cornbread and pinto beans and chicken-fried steak and gravy; and he took his plate to the kitchen sink without being told. But other than that, he acted like he belonged. He took a shower in the basement, teased my little sister who's three years younger than I am, and strummed on my old guitar which I can't play very well.

I was glad for that. My folks never said anything much about it, but they just acted like they trusted me more after he came than they did before. I never had much trouble that way anyhow, but it is just a lot easier to have your folks act like they trust you. You don't have to have as good a memory because you don't have to answer a lot of questions.

Chuck and I worked some that fall. I didn't intend for that to happen and I was kind of surprised the way it all turned out. I'd worked around Wheatheart quite a lot for years, driving tractors, plowing, working cattle, things like that. It keeps me in gas money and Levi's and I give what is left to my mom sometimes. Well, Mr. Granger down at the Co-op elevator asked me if I wanted to help run his wheat-cleaning machine. I said I could if he would run it late enough for me to work after school. Not only did he set it up that way, but he even allowed me enough time to run first. I don't think he knew I was running, but I was glad it worked out that way.

The wheat-cleaning machine is a portable rig which we take out to a farmer's place. We park it by the granary and scoop in wheat. Then the machine shakes and blows the wheat until it sifts all the weed seed and stems and other junk out so the clean seed will run through the drills easy. We then scoop it back into the granary, stopping once in a while to mix in some awful-smelling, purple dust bug killer.

Now that may not sound like a very important job, but it is something that has to be done, so it makes you feel good to do it. Once in a while in the spring when the wheat is really beginning to grow and the whole country is turning deep green, I drive by some of those farms and look at the growth, and just say to myself, "I helped clean that seed." It makes me feel like I am part of farming.

Well, the first afternoon I was going to work, I mentioned to Chuck that I was in a hurry and told him why. He asked if I thought he might get a job too. I didn't know about that. First, I never figured that he wanted to work, and then I just couldn't see him scooping grain out of some old boarded-up, weather-beaten grana-ry, him with his buckskin hair and bronze skin and Nike shoes. It wasn't like the beaches of California, not with the dust blowing in your face and that purple junk in your mouth and throat and your back hurting from bending over and scooping. But I told him I would check anyway.

Well, sure enough, Mr. Granger hired him too and he went out with me. I was kind of hoping he wouldn't. I was afraid I was going to have to do both of our jobs. But I didn't. At first, he didn't know much about scooping, but after I showed him, he learned quick. From then on, he stood right beside me and matched me scoopful for scoopful. In fact, I sometimes had to stop and wipe sweat, but he never did, or at least I never saw him. Sometimes in order to finish a job so the farmer could sow the next day, we would work late into the night. Our hands would blister and our backs would get sore and our eyes would be all red from the dust, and our throats burned from the purple stuff, and I would look over at Chuck working in the Oklahoma fall moonlight, and he would look back, crinkle his eyes and just keep on scooping. I liked him more every day.

I think we both felt a little more grown-up when we were working. Part of it might have been the money, but it was more than that. Someone was depending on us to do a job, and knowing that made us work harder.

Of course, we did take time off on Friday nights to go to the football games, but that was kind of hard work too. We started by going to the Watonga game, since we felt we'd had something to do with it. We stood on the sidelines and cheered as our Whippets, playing like they were mad at somebody, whipped those Eagles 27-7.

After the game, everybody congratulated each other for such a fine victory. I smiled some, but Chuck just crinkled his eyes.

After that, we went to the games, but we didn't really belong. In some towns where football isn't the most important thing, they let the high school guys who don't play run the down box and the chains. That way, at least, those guys feel like they are welcome to come and watch. But not in Wheatheart. We have a couple old guys who have been doing that job for thirty years or more. If you want to run something at a Wheatheart football game, you have to live until one of them dies, and neither of us had lived that long.

We couldn't sit with the pep club either, because we would be the only two guys in the whole group, except for seventh and eighth graders. Besides we made the girls nervous. Even if they wanted to talk to us, they really never acted like they felt too good doing it.

We tried walking alond the sidelines with the old guys, birddogs the players called them, but that didn't work either. Although everybody in town knew what was wrong with me, and they could accept the fact that I didn't play, they never understood Chuck; so they stared at him a lot—not mean or anything, but just curious enough to make him feel like he really didn't belong.

So we mostly stood by ourselves in one end zone and watched the best we could from a distance. Chuck knew a lot more about the game than I thought he would—a lot more than I knew, even though I had played—so he helped me watch better. I really enjoyed that season. In fact, I enjoyed the whole fall.

"Last One In Buys"

By the second week in November, the football watching was still good, but the wheat sowing had turned sour. The team was undefeated, but we hadn't had rain. It was dry, dryest I had ever seen. Of course, for my folks and the old-timers around town, it was just dry enough to remind them of the old days when it was really dry. In some places, people talk about the "good old days" all the time. But not in Wheatheart. Here everybody seems to like to tell about the "bad old days."

"Dirtiest I ever seen it."

"Wettest I ever seen it."

"Worst tornado I ever seen."

Well, when they start talking about the dryest and the dustiest bad old days, they all have stories to tell.

"Chickens went to roost at noon!"

"Street lights came on at two in the afternoon!"

"Dust silted into new cars!"

"Sand blew so deep it covered up a plow left out in the field!"

It wasn't *that* bad, but it was still the worst I'd ever seen. There was a dusty haze in the sky which made everything look eerie and a long way off. Some days when we ran, we couldn't even see the hills along the river. But even then, Chuck found reasons to marvel at things.

"Look at the dust way up there in the sky. There doesn't seem to be any wind. How does it stay suspended like that?"

"Those hills really take on a lot of different tints through the dust, red and brown and purple."

"Notice how the new-plowed dirt draws the sand to it like a magnet. I wonder why that is."

I had never thought about it, but I started once he mentioned it to me.

One Thursday afternoon, the second week in November, we ran out the first mile as usual, chattering away about the dust and the colors and schoolwork and things like that. It was just one of those days when you feel good running and being together. Just after we turned around, and started back, Chuck got real serious and said, "Last one in buys," and he took off as fast as he could run. Well, he took me by surprise. By the time I got into high gear, he was already maybe ten yards ahead, far enough for me to admire his style. He can really run, beautiful form, head held erect, legs reaching out and coming back swift, body in control everywhere. Well, I ran behind him like that for at least three-quarters of the way in. I really wasn't losing much distance but I wasn't gaining either. Although I was running past my comfortable speed, I did it because I wanted to stay close enough to study him. I ran out of breath a bit, got a little dizzy and felt jellylike in my legs, but other than that I was doing all right. I figured I could probably even finish at that speed.

For some reason, while we were still a quarter of a mile away from the Whippet, I started picturing myself running like Chuck. While I was thinking that thought, it just came to me that I could really run faster than I was. I don't know why I thought that, because on any other day, I wouldn't have believed it, but not this day. So I just decided to take off, and I did. All of a sudden, I forgot the pain and the thin air and I was running easier and wilder than I ever had before. I started reaching way out with my legs and my breathing got together with the rest of me. To my surprise, I started gaining on him. At first, I couldn't believe it—*I was gaining*. I thought it just looked that way. But after a few more steps, I realized I really was gaining, so I ran even harder and I gained even more. I just kept running and gaining until I came right up alongside him. He looked over at me, crinkled his eyes, then looked straight ahead again. We ran side by side like that for a long time. Although I didn't see him do it, I figured he must have speeded up some when he saw me coming.

But maybe fifty yards from the Whippet, I looked over again, and he wasn't there. I didn't dare look back to see how far behind he was. I just looked straight ahead and kept on running, thinking he would come whizzing by anytime. But he never did. I ran right past the Whippet and right past the old Chevy and almost out on the Highway before I could get everything slowed down and under control enough to stop. But when I did, I turned around, and there he was standing at the corner of the Whippet, feet spread apart, head bent down, arms dangling past his head almost to the ground. I walked over to him, staggered actually, panting and gasping. He looked up at me and didn't say a word. When I finally got enough air to speak, I said, as best I could, telling and asking at the same time, "You let me win?"

He crinkled his eyes and looked at me for a long time before he answered, "Don't bet on it." Then he looked at me some more and said, "We'll drink small limeades tonight."

10

"Keep Running, Osgood!"

The next day I felt good all day, partly because it was Friday, partly because it was the last regular season football game and the team was undefeated. But mostly I felt good because I had run faster than I ever knew I could. Even if Chuck let me win, I still felt good about what I had done.

I didn't tell anyone. I didn't even brag to Chuck at study hall about beating him. But I just went through the day feeling good and thinking that I could do more than I'd ever thought I could.

I was still feeling good that afternoon when we got back out to the Whippet to run, but not good enough to expect his next move. As we were getting stripped down and limbered up, he said real matter-of-fact, just as if it were an everyday matter, "Today we run to the cemetery."

"What?" I had heard what he said, but didn't want to believe it.

"We run all the way to the cemetery." He said it again the same way.

"How do we get back?" I raised my voice like a real question.

"We run. What do you think?" He was still calm.

"That's six miles," I said, as if he were still a stranger and didn't understand such things. "I can't run six miles. Some days I can't even drive six miles. Human beings just aren't made to run six miles. It makes your heart grow too big, running like that."

He didn't say anything. He just crinkled his eyes and said, "You're all right, Osgood," and he took off running his normal pace.

I followed, but I complained about it. It didn't do any good. He just kept running. The first mile wasn't bad. That was just like we had been running. The second mile wasn't bad either, although it seemed a little strange to be that far from the cherry limeades and the old Chevy. Then we started the third mile, still going out toward the cemetery, and I was almost surprised when my legs didn't fall off or my heart didn't stop beating or anything bad. Isn't it funny how we tell ourselves we can do just so much and nothing more? Then when we find out we can do more, we are surprised by the discovery. Well, that was the way I was that day. Not only did I keep running, but I even enjoyed it, once I got over my fright of doing it. As we ran that third mile, the hills up along the river just seemed to grow out of the dust in the air, different from how I had ever seen them before. For a long time, I ran that third mile looking at the hills and watching them grow as we got closer, and I forgot to think that we were running farther than I ever had before.

By the time we got to the cemetery and turned around, we were both running smooth and rather easy, and we had fallen into a good silence, just running side by side, looking and thinking and not saying anything. I decided to speak. "Ever know why they built such a big fence around the cemetery out here?"

"No," he said, like he thought he was about to learn something.

"Because people were just dying to get in." I knew it was an old joke, but I didn't know whether he had ever heard it or not.

He didn't laugh. He just said, "Keep running, Osgood."

For some reason which I still don't know, I wished I hadn't said it. But we kept running. We ran the first mile back and about half way through the second mile, I suddenly realized, right in the middle of a step, that we were going to run all the way in. I was going to make it! I was going to run six miles! I would have run all the way to the cemetery and back! Well, after I realized that, there was no stopping me. Oh, my feet got sore and my legs a little wobbly, and my head hurt just a bit, and I sweated more than usual, especially for that nippy of a day. But I knew I was going to do it. I knew I could finish.

And we did finish, step by step, side by side. We bought our own jumbo cherry limeades, sat with our feet dangling off the Chevy tailgate, sipped real slow because we knew the football players wouldn't come on a Friday, and talked about running to the cemetery and back.

That night at the football game, the last regular of the season, I stood in the end zone with Chuck, put my hand in my pocket, stood as tall as I could, and felt different than I had ever felt before. I was happy, but I didn't know why. I was important, but for no reason, and especially for no reason that anybody else would care about. I hadn't really changed—I was the same person. But inside I was different and only I knew it.

As usual, the Whippets made short work of Shattuck. The game was all but over at halftime, but they played on anyway—through the night and through the dust, the players played on as if they had something to prove to the world, and the people watched as if it really mattered. Somewhere near the end of the game, and it doesn't matter where, Wheatheart ran the ball around right end for a short gain. As usual, I watched Scotty Garland, the quarterback, run, and I missed all the action in the middle of the line. But that was all right, because Chuck watched everything and he would tell me if I missed something exciting. After the tackle, I looked back into the center of the line and saw a bunch of guys gathered around. Chuck must have felt me looking because he answered my question before I asked. "Jimmy Charles is hurt. It looks bad."

But as it turned out, he wasn't hurt after all. He was dead. It was a freaky thing, we found out later. He just got hit in the right place and a blood vessel in his brain broke. In the middle of the football field, Jimmy Charles was dead.

11

A *Right* To *Live*

I didn't sleep well that night. I didn't understand death at all. Jimmy Charles was the first person I knew who had died. Well, of course, there was my grandaddy and my great uncle and old Mr. Baker and people like that. But this was the first time someone I was used to being around and expected to see again, someone who talked like me and with me, had died—had just disappeared—and I didn't know where he was or what was happening.

But that wasn't what bothered me. I was sad, the saddest I had ever been in my life. I would just wake up in the middle of the night and for no reason at all, tears would come into my eyes. I didn't understand that either, but that wasn't what bothered me.

What really bothered me was that I had been so happy, the happiest I had ever been in my life, and ten minutes later I was the saddest I had ever been, and that bothered me. It sounded like something Brother Bob would make sermon out of, the unexpected things in life. But all that is true, I guess. When you are happy, you had better be happy you are happy, because the next minute you may be sad, and through no cause of your own.

I got up early the next morning and drove out to the Ericson farm. I don't know why I did except that Jimmy Charles was their only kid and I knew they would have an even bigger empty spot than I did. But I still didn't know what I would say. I tried practicing something before I got there, but nothing came out very good. The truth is I almost cried when I thought of something I liked well enough to say. I was sort of mad at myself for going, me with nothing to say. I knew there would be a big crowd of grown-ups, all with the right things to say.

When I got there, there was a crowd all right, but nobody was talking much. They were all just standing around having about as much trouble as I was. I went over to Mrs. Ericson first. I didn't know what to say, so I hugged her. I don't know why I did that. I never have hugged any woman in the world except my mom, and I don't do that as much as I should. But I hugged Jimmy Charles' mom hard and long, right there in her own living room. She didn't say anything either, but she hugged me back. Then I went out to the other room, found his dad and hugged him too. I don't think I was supposed to do that. I think I was supposed to shake his hand and look sad. That is what everyone else was doing. But I hugged him, and he hugged back too.

I didn't say a word. I just hugged them both. I guess, someday when I get a lot smarter, I'll know what to say in times like these and I won't have to go around just hugging people. But that day it was all I knew to do.

I went home, got out my old shotgun and drove up into the hills along the river to do some rabbit hunting. In the past, I had done that when I was happy, and I thought the same thing might work when I was sad. But it didn't help much. For a while I just walked along, not thinking anything—just being. When the first old jackrabbit jumped up and started to lope off kind of slow, I pulled up the shotgun and was going to blast him. But I stopped before I did and thought how silly that was. Here I was, so sad because someone had died, and I was about to kill something else to make me feel better. That didn't make any sense. That rabbit had a right to live. So I took the shells out of my 12-gauge and just walked and thought.

I knew Jimmy Charles before we even started to school. I used to go down to the elevator with my dad when times were slow and Jimmy Charles would come with his dad; then while our dads stood and talked, the two of us would run around the elevator and play in the wheat. When he first started to school, he and I still played a lot at recess and we never fought like other kids that age. In junior high, we even had a couple of classes together and I sat behind him because his name began with E and mine with G. Even though he played football, he was always friendly and easy to talk to; but when we talked, we always talked about me. We never talked about him. When I went to church for the first time that morning three years ago, just to show off the old Chevy, I went to the Baptist Church because I knew Jimmy Charles would be there, and I thought that if anybody had religion, really had it so it showed, he did.

But now he was dead. I didn't know what that meant for sure, but I knew I would never see him again, and I knew he would never play football again, or run the combine, or write poetry. Although I don't know what it is like, I know there is a heaven, and I know Jimmy Charles is there. But I think for me, I would still rather be alive than dead.

That afternoon, when I got home, Brother Bob called and asked if I would be a pallbearer at the funeral on Monday. I said I would, but I also told him that because of Osgood in my left elbow, I would have to lift on the right side of the casket. He said that wouldn't be a problem.

That night when I thought everybody was in bed, I was just lying there staring at the ceiling and strumming my old guitar, trying to figure out how people get music out of those things, when my mom walked in. She didn't knock or anything. She just walked in. I was afraid I was going to get it for waking her up, and felt bad about it. Instead, she just crept over, bent down, hugged me, and left again. I don't know what she meant by it, but I put the guitar up anyway.

Monday we didn't have school. They turned it out completely for Jimmy Charles' funeral. My dad said that once before, years ago, somebody had died in a car wreck and Casteel refused to turn out school for it. He wondered why it was different this time, but maybe my dad didn't know about Jimmy Charles that much.

Being a pallbearer was easier than I thought it would be. The casket was already at the front of the church when we got there so we just marched in, five football players and me, and we sat together on the front pew. All the rest of the football team marched in and sat together right in the middle of the church. Chuck told me later that he thought it was awful showy, but I explained to him that at Wheatheart you have to do those things, especially when people expect you to. It doesn't hurt anything to do what people expect you to do if it's as easy as not doing it.

The girls' trio sang "In the Garden," and I listened because Connie Faye sings the low voice. But somewhere in the middle, I realized that I didn't like that song very much and I don't think Jimmy Charles would have liked it at all. After that, Brother Bob preached, but I didn't listen much—I was too busy thinking about other things.

When that was over and everybody had passed by the casket, we carried it out and loaded it in the hearse. Then we all six got in that old blue Lincoln funeral car and drove out to the cemetery. On the way out, the football players talked about whether they would have practice that night and who they were going to play in the first game of the bye-district. I just sat by the door and looked out the window and tried to remember the time I once ran all the way out to the cemetery. But it seemed so long ago that I quit trying.

We buried him over by the elm tree in northeast corner. After that, every time we ran by the cemetery, or even drove by, I would slow down and look over to that spot. I know he isn't there. He's in heaven, wherever that is, but I look just the same. It reminds me not to be too proud of myself, no matter what I do. And it reminds me not to tell jokes about dead people anymore.

12

Tears in My Eyes

I didn't go to the dinner after the funeral. I guess I should have, with me being one of the officials and all, but it just didn't seem right. I know those people meant well, and it was all right for them to go and eat and laugh. But for me, it was like throwing a party for somebody who couldn't come, and I just couldn't see anything fair about that.

I went home and worked around the house some. I changed the oil in the old Chevy and washed it real good now that the seed-cleaning days were over. After a long time, it got to be four-thirty and I thought about running. Since I hadn't talked with Chuck since Friday night, I didn't know whether he would want to go or not, but I decided to go myself anyway. I put on my stuff and drove by his house. He was sitting on the porch waiting for me, and he came jogging out like he knew I would be there. We drove out to the Whippet and got ready to run. That afternoon we didn't even fuss about where we were going. We just knew we were going to the cemetery. Last Friday seemed so long ago that I could barely remember it, except for being scared I couldn't run that far. But I wasn't that Monday afternoon. I knew what I could do and I didn't worry about it anymore. It was almost like I was somebody else, and didn't know how I got that way.

We ran and talked about everything we could think of which didn't matter much. First we added up how many times we had run that first mile already that fall—seventy-two times round-trip. We had the road about memorized and started betting on how many steps to the next crack in the pavement or which thistle was the one with the branch missing—silly stuff like that. Next, we each took a turn at running funny and making the other one copy. We ran backward, we took real long steps, we ran with our legs stiff like German soldiers, and we ran as fast as we could without moving our arms. It was all fun, and on any other day it would have tired me out some.

After that, we each went to opposite sides of the road, picked up dirt clods off the side of the bank and threw them at each other. Since we were kind of close together for a clod fight, we had to change speeds a lot to keep from getting hit. With my good arm, I could throw better than he did, but he could dodge better than I did, so we were about evenly matched.

When we got out to the cemetery, we forgot about being silly for a while and we both came back into the middle of the road and ran together. I probably imagined it, but it seemed that we ran closer than usual. I tried not think about anything and I don't know what he was thinking. Finally, he asked, rather quiet, "Do you ever think about death?"

"Nope," I answered sooner than I wished I had. "Only in church when that is what you are supposed to think about." He didn't say anything, so I talked again. "The preacher talks about death a lot and what happens when you die and how to get ready for it." I waited again, but he still didn't say anything. After a while I just asked him, "Do you ever go to church much?"

"Nope," he said and sounded like he wished I hadn't asked, but I didn't pay any attention.

"Why not?"

"People don't ever seem to laugh much in church." He said it like he had his eyes crinkled, but I couldn't tell.

"They're not supposed to." I told him like I was a real expert. "They go to church to talk about God and death and heaven and love and things like that. It isn't supposed to be funny stuff."

"Well, if it's any good, it ought to make them feel better." he said, as if he was serious.

"It does." I might have sounded impatient.

"So why don't they laugh?" he asked, as if he had me trapped with his logic.

"It's an inner peace," I said, like I knew all about it. After going a few steps more, I just blurted out, "Why don't you come with me Sunday and find out for yourself?"

"I couldn't go to church," he said. "I wouldn't know how to act."

"You don't act in church," I was beginning to sound like a mother talking to her baby. "You just sit there and listen and don't do anything."

"I wouldn't know how to listen." I guess he was being a hard case. This was the first time I had ever asked anybody to go to church and I didn't know how they were supposed to turn me down.

But I thought of something else to say. "What do you mean, you wouldn't know how to listen? You just sit there with your ears open and listen. That's all there is to it."

Now it was his time. "I wouldn't know what all the words mean."

"That's dumb. They use the same words in church that they use anywhere else." Then I thought about what I had just said, and decided it wasn't quite true. If it had been somebody else, I might have quit there; but since it was Chuck and we had been through so much already, I decided that I had better tell him. "Well, I guess they do have some special words that you ought to know if you want to understand everything."

"Like what?" he sounded interested.

"Well, like baptize, for example. Usually when they talk about baptize, it means dunking you into water, but then sometimes the preacher asks if we have been baptized by fire, and I don't know what that means."

"See?" He acted as if he had just made his point.

I went on anyway. "They also have a bunch of names for eating the crackers and the grape juice. Sometimes they call it Communion and sometimes they call it the Lord's Supper, and I think the Catholics even have another name for it, a real old and religious sounding name." This time he didn't say anything, so I went on. "You have to understand sin too."

"Yeah?" he said. "Just exactly what is sin?"

"Well, according to what I hear Brother Bob say, sin is anything that makes God mad."

"So what does God get mad about?" He wasn't teasing me, and that was a hard question.

"I guess that depends on who you talk to," I said. "Some people think God gets mad at you if you take a little drink, but others don't feel that way. Dancing is something else they don't agree on. I guess it all depends."

"That's my problem," he interrupted me. "When people explain sin to me, it seems to be anything that I do that they don't do, that they think I shouldn't do."

I thought about that for a while. I knew it wasn't right, but I couldn't figure out what was wrong with it, so I decided to go another direction. "Yes, but there is more than that. Take sacrifice."

"I know what sacrifice is," he interrupted again.

"What?" I thought he was serious.

"It's when there is a man on first and you make an out so he can go to second."

With that I dropped the subject. After we quit talking, we both just naturally speeded up a bit and we ran a long ways. Although it was still dry, the dust and wind had settled a bit, and I could see the town a lot clearer, so I looked hard trying to see something I had never seen before. After we had really gotten into running, I tried doing that every day. That afternoon, I noticed that over on the Eckhart elevator, the big E up on that little doghouse on top was not as big on the east side as it was on the north. I know that isn't any big deal, but I had fun wondering how it happened. While I was doing that, Chuck said, almost so soft I couldn't hear, "Where is he now?"

I ran along for several yards, watching my feet hit the pavement and making sure I knew for sure. "In heaven." I said it soft, but I was sure.

After a few more yards, he said, "Okay, come by. I'll go Sunday."

I ran a while trying to decide whether I was happy because he was going or because I had won the argument. I really hoped it was the first. I wanted to make him feel good about deciding to go, so I said, "Let me tell you a story," and I looked over at him. He just shook his head, but he crinkled his eyes, so I went on. "This little boy invited his friend to church, but the friend didn't want to go because he wouldn't understand anything. The little boy said that he would explain it all as they went along. Well, the preacher stood up and kneeled by the pulpit. The friend said, 'What's that mean?' The little boy said, 'Shh, he's going to pray.' Then the preacher got up and opened the big Bible on the pulpit. The friend said, 'What's that mean?' The little boy whispered back, 'Quiet, we're going to read the Scripture.' Then, when he was finished reading, the preacher took out his watch and laid it on the pulpit. The friend asked, 'What does that mean?' The little boy said, 'Nothing.' "

I ran along waiting for him to laugh but he didn't. So I looked over to see if he even knew I was finished telling the story. He crinkled his eyes and said, "Just run, Osgood. At least you're good at that."

The next day I got a note from Jimmy Charles' mom. It read "Delbert, I can't tell you how much your visit meant to me last Saturday. Thank you for being man enough to hug me." She had signed it just, "Mary Ruth."

I didn't know what to make of it. No one had ever called me a man before, and all I had done was hug her because I didn't know what else to do. If that is the way men are supposed to act, a lot of men I know don't know it.

Oh, well, I liked the note. But I still got tears in my eyes when I woke up at night thinking about Jimmy Charles.

13

Afraid To Remember Out Loud

Every day that week Chuck and I ran all the way to the cemetery and back. By Saturday, we were even comfortable enough with it that we raced all the way back in. He beat me, but not by as much as I thought he might. Since I lost, I just naturally went up to the Whippet window by myself and bought two small limeades while he dangled his feet off the tailgate of the old Chevy. He didn't laugh or gripe or anything. He just crinkled his eyes and sipped slowly.

On Friday night, the football team beat Laverne to win the bye-district, and on Sunday Chuck and I went to church. He dressed up more than I expected, more than most of us ever do, but with him it was different. When he dressed up, he didn't look uncomfortable and he didn't fidget with things the way I do. Everybody was really friendly to him too—the kids and the grown-ups, and Brother Bob even knew his name before I told him. I thought that should make Chuck feel welcome.

When we walked in, though, he did notice the cigarette butts out by the front step. "Looks worse than the halls of my old high school out in California," was all that he said, but he might have said more. A lot of our men in the church do go outside and smoke between Sunday School and church, but I had never really noticed how the

74

butts piled up until Chuck said that.

The Sunday School lesson that morning was a good one, or at least I thought it was good. It was taken from over in Matthew where Christ goes out in the wilderness and fasts and prays for forty days and nights. Then Satan comes and tempts Him with all sorts of things, but Christ won't give in. I like that story. It shows that we can fight off temptation, no matter how strong it is. We just have to stick to what we know is right. I do think our teacher is good. Since she is Scotty Garland's mom, she knows kids and she seems to like them. Since her husband travels a lot selling tractors and doing business, she has time to read books and study her lesson. She does wear a little too much makeup to suit me, but I figure that is her business.

That day we read about how Christ didn't have anything to eat or drink for forty days and forty nights. I can't imagine that, but He was Christ so He could do it if He wanted to. But then, Old Satan came and tempted Him with food. Scotty's mom said that it would look like Satan came at Christ's weakest moment, His being so hungry and all. But she said that wasn't true. Christ was in a strong mood because He had been fasting and praying all the time. "We make ourselves strong through worship," she said, and I thought about that the next time we went running.

Now don't get the idea that I remember that much about all Sunday School lessons, even if I do have a good teacher. This was a special day. Chuck was with me so I listened more than I usually do, and I listened because of some other things that had happened that week too.

But we did have a distraction. Carol Ann Reinschimdt, a sophomore who goes with senior football players, came in late and sat down in front of me and Chuck. She had a big hickey on her neck where somebody had kissed her too hard the night before. I tried to look the other way and not see it, but I couldn't. I would have thought she might have tried to hide it, but she didn't. She wore a low-cut dress as if she wanted to show it off.

Chuck and I both saw it at the same time, and we had to work to keep from giggling out loud. That was the first time I have ever seen him giggle or even need to.

Church went fairly smoothly, for us at least. I don't know how other churches are, but I like our church because nobody gets upset if something doesn't go quite right. Oh, before church, we had the normal conversations around in all the corners. A couple of mothers were yakking at Mr. Benalli because he wouldn't let the cheerleaders out of school early to get ready for the football game, and the two women in front of us were gossiping about why somebody named "they" let Scotty's mom teach Sunday School, when she couldn't bring her own husband to church with her. But these are all such a part of our church that you wouldn't know they were going on if you didn't know what to look for. I hoped Chuck didn't notice, but he probably did. He was really looking around like he thought everything was interesting.

During the offering, right in the middle of a piano solo by Scotty's little sister, a little kid behind us dropped the collection plate and spilled money all down Chuck's back. He just crinkled his eyes and picked money up from off the pew and off the floor and put it back into the plate. Then he bent over real close and whispered, "Do we take Communion today?"

I whispered back trying to be quiet so nobody would hear me, "No."

"Good," he whispered, and went back to listening.

Brother Bob's sermon was pretty good that day, but maybe not quite as good as usual. He talked about belonging to the family of God, and he told us about all the lonely people in the world who don't belong to anything or anybody and how lucky we were that we had each other, being of like mind as we were. He must have got excited about the whole thing because he did go past noon. When it was over and we were walking out, Chuck bent over and said, so only I would hear, "Your story is funnier than I thought it was, Osgood."

I just said back, "Do you want to come to my house for dinner?" He said, "Sure."

When we got to my house, my mom was in the kitchen finishing dinner. She asked us how we liked church, and Chuck started telling her about it. He sat down on the kitchen stool, over by the refrigerator out of the way, put his feet up on the second rung, and told her all about it. I went into my room and changed clothes; when I came back, they were still there talking about church and God. I never knew what they said. I guess if I had wanted to know, I could have stayed in the kitchen myself. But then they probably wouldn't have said it and I still wouldn't ever know.

After dinner, we went to my room, did some homework, strummed on the old guitar, and took naps, Chuck on the bed and me on the floor. But we didn't even think about going running. We had settled that a long time ago.

Only one thing bothered me about that day, though. In all the church time, Sunday School and church both, nobody said anything about Jimmy Charles. We just treated him like he was on a vacation somewhere. Even worse. If he had been on vacation, we would have mentioned it and prayed for him. But it seemed like we just forgot him. Oh, I am sure some people stopped by and talked to his mom and dad, but nobody said anything official. No, on second thought, it didn't seem as if we had forgot him. He was there all right, at least his memory was, just underneath what we really talked abut. But it seemed like we were afraid to remember out loud—afraid to think about it.

14

Looking Straight Ahead

That's the way it was for the next two weeks. Wheatheart had more
to do than think of death, even if it was in the back of our minds.
We had to win the state championship in football. And I guess that
is important, even though we had won it the year before and a lot of
years before then. Winning is always better than losing.

That's what makes our town special. Oh, we have good wheat
some years, and we have people who have money, and we have
Moss Bosco, the artist who wears a funny little cap and paints signs
on all the buildings. But other than that we are pretty average—
except for our football team. Maybe that is the problem—we don't
want to be average. We want to be the best, so we put all our hopes
on the football team. When the team wins, we are the best, and
when the team doesn't win, we go back to being average, and act a
little grumpy about it.

We really don't have much else to build a reputation on. We don't
have any crooks, so we don't get attention that way. We haven't
even had a tornado right in town since I can remember, and that in
itself makes us unusual for this part of Oklahoma.

Nope, when we are trying to win the state championship, everyone in town spends most of his time just looking straight ahead. We

don't have much energy to look back or think of the past, unless, of course, it is the distant past and includes football. Those guys in the old days must have been really good, lots better than we are today. At least, that's the idea you get when you hear people tell it.

But Jimmy Charles wasn't the only one who got ignored. So did Chuck and I. Nobody has much to do with you when they have other things on their minds and you are not part of those things. By that time in the season, the football players all had little jokes on each other which were only funny to them. The cheerleaders and all the other girls in school started acting like *they* had won all the games up to that point, and were more important than the players themselves. They spent most of their time fighting with each other and the teachers. The teachers were just trying to survive and didn't want to talk to anyone they didn't have to.

The people downtown in the stores had Moss Bosco paint "Win State, Whippets" on their front windows and then just stood around on the stoops for two weeks and chatted about football, future and past. Even Earl Bresserman got into the act. He drove around at night keeping tabs on the football players, trying to make sure they didn't get drunk or do something else to embarrass the town.

This year seemed different than the other years we won State because this was Coach Rose's last year to coach. He had been at Wheatheart a long time, more than twenty years, anyway. I know he coached Scotty Garland's dad and Jimmy Charles' dad and some of the other old-timers around.

I didn't know why he was quitting for sure. I guess he just got tired. I think I understood that much. Since we had won so many football games, the town acted as if they thought he was really something; but he didn't ever act like he thought he was. He was always friendlier to me than I was to him. Since everybody in town thought that the only thing he ever thought about was football, I never knew what to talk to him about. But he could always find some reason to talk to me. Even years after I had quit football and it didn't matter anymore, he asked about my elbow, or he would ask me about my seed-cleaning job, or just stop to tell me a story. He was good at that. One time during our sophomore year when our English class was reading something from a guy named Plutarch, Coach Rose came into our room and talked about the Romans for the whole period. He knew a lot about them and he made the story really interesting. Even though I didn't play football and didn't know the coach like the rest of the guys did, I still liked him a lot, and I did want the team to win.

I told this to Chuck one afternoon while we were running out to the cemetery. It was on Wednesday before the championship game with Hartshorne. We were talking about the game and the school and the town and how nobody had really talked to us or even noticed us for the past two weeks. While I was thinking about it, I decided that complaining too much might sound like I wasn't loyal, and I did want to be loyal. So I told Chuck that I really wanted the team to win, even though I didn't always act like it. He said he did too, and we ran along for a while not saying anything. Then he said, "We're going to have to help them."

"What?" By then I was running rather serious-like and didn't hear him.

"We're just going to have to help them. We helped them win the first game. Now we need to help them win the last game. It's our civic duty." I laughed out loud and almost got out of step when I remembered our part in the first game, but he just crinkled his eyes.

I decided he was serious. "What do we do this time?"

"I don't know," and he stopped talking to think. "How do you make a football player mad?"

"Steal his girl." I hadn't had any experience, but I thought that would work.

"No," he said. "Not mad that way, but mad enough to play inspired."

"Call him a sissy." It sounded dumb, but I had to say something while I was stalling for time.

"That's it," he jumped in right away. "That's what we will do."

"Not me." I stopped him. "I'm not about to call those guys sissies. They lift weights, and besides, I got a hurt elbow."

"But you can outrun them, Osgood." He said it and didn't even crinkle his eyes. I had never really thought about it until then. I knew I could run six miles and I knew I could run faster than I ever thought I could, but it had never occurred to me that I could outrun somebody, even football players. I wanted to think about that, but I didn't have time right then. He went on without me asking him to. "Can we get into the dressing room?"

"When?" I wished I hadn't asked.

"Tomorrow night." He had something definite in mind.

"Sure," I told him. "They just have one of those slide locks on the door. We can slip it with a screwdriver and. . . ."

"Good." He didn't let me finish.

"What do you have in mind?" I knew it wouldn't hurt anybody, but I still wanted to know.

"I'll tell you then. Just pick me up tomorrow night about eight," and that is all he would say.

That next day was tough, but fun too. We didn't really have that much schoolwork. Everybody was so excited, making plans and bragging about what we were going to do. Mr. Benalli tried to keep us calm and in class, but even he couldn't do it. Everybody had something important to do and somewhere important to go— except Chuck and me. We just sat in class all day. We did talk to each other during study hall, but not about the plan. He wasn't saying anything and I wasn't asking, even though I wanted to.

For the last hour of the day, they turned out school for a pep rally downtown. We marched down Main Street, all the students and even some of the teachers. We went down to the John Deere store, where they had parked a semi in the middle of the street. By the time we got there, a big crowd had gathered with people standing on the sidewalks and some leaning out the stores. All the big shots in town took turns talking on the loudspeaker, telling us how proud they were of the football team and how much they appreciated all the hard work and blood and sweat and how this was a real town victory-stuff like that. Then Coach Rose got up, acting a little embarrassed, and had each of the football players come up one by one. Most of them were rather sensible about it, but some of them made gestures, like waving their fists, and the crowd would cheer. Then Coach Rose made a little speech which sounded humble. He said that victory is always the result of some unknown ingredient, some cause powerful enough to carry us past pain to the victory. I liked that speech. Chuck must have too, because he just looked at me and crinkled his eyes.

I picked him up at eight like we had planned. I still didn't know what he had in mind, but after that rally, I was inspired enough to do anything that would help. When he came out to get in the old Chevy, he was carrying a paper sack. I could tell he had a bottle in it, but I didn't know what in the bottle. I just figured he would tell me when he got ready.

We drove up the west side of town to the half-mile road which runs north of the football field. Then we parked the old Chevy, got out, and lay on the bank, looking up at the sky. Although there was still some dust in the air, it was a clear night, and the stars and the moon were all over the sky, almost close enough to touch in places. Now, I knew the stars and the moon were bright in Oklahoma that time of the fall, but I had never just laid on my back and looked at them. But I did that night and saw things I had never really seen before. Chuck pointed them out to me, not the usual things like the Big dipper and the Little Dipper, but the other things too, like the Seven Dancing Sisters.

Pretty soon, he said it was time to go, but I wasn't really ready. I could have stayed and looked at the stars all night, I guess. We jogged up the road, slow and easy so nobody would hear us, climbed the fence at the football field, sneaked across, and went around behind the bleachers to the dressing room. I handed him the screwdriver, and he had the door open before I could even turn back around. We sneaked in and closed the door behind us. The moon came through the windows so clear that we could still see our shadows, even inside. Chuck said, "Do you know where the seniors dress?"

I said, "Sure." I would know that, of course, because at

Wheatheart everything is done by custom. For all the years I can remember, the seniors have dressed over in the far corner. They have the best benches and the best lockers and the best outside hooks. It's all part of the program. When you start as a freshman, you get a locker by the door, and you share hooks, but as you get older, you move toward that corner. When you get to be a senior, you get to dress there, even if you aren't a starter.

We went over to the senior lockers, where they had their shoulder pads hanging on the outside hooks, letting the sweat dry off so they would be ready to pack for the trip to the City and the championship game the next day.

Chuck then took the bottle out of the sack. In the moonlight, I couldn't read what it was, but he took the cap off and let me smell. It was perfume, real strong and smelly. He said that his mother had got that whole big bottle as a trick gift somewhere once at a party, and he had kept it for just such an occasion. We sprinkled that stuff over all eleven sets of the seniors' shoulder pads. We wanted to rub it in, but we were afraid to get it on ourselves, so we just sprinkled and hoped it would soak in enough to still smell the next day.

After we finished, we stood by the door awhile. I didn't know how long it would last, but right then, that place smelled worse than the room at church where they have the women's meetings.

The next day, we got out of school at noon. Chuck and I went out and ran; then we got in the old Chevy and drove to the City to see the state championship football game. We sat up high in the stands and watched the Whippets beat Hartshorne 31-0. When the game was over, we walked past some Wheatheart big shots and old-timers who were congratulating themselves for the victory and bragging abut how good the pep rally was the day before. I looked at Chuck. He just crinkled his eyes. When we got out to the bus, all the sophomore football players were standing there in a straight line at attention with their hands over their heads. We asked one of the seniors what was going on. He told us they were being punished for something they had done; but since he didn't act like he wanted to talk about it, we didn't ask any questions.

A Christmas To Remember

W i n t e r 1 9 8 1 - 1 9 8 2

After the wheat is sowed and the maize is all cut and the last football game is played, winter comes to Wheatheart. Usually, we only get a few days of real winter, but since they are scattered out over three months, the worst part is never the cold and snow, but dreading it.

Even though it's bad enough out on the wheatfields and the prairie, it's even worse in school. You just aren't supposed to enjoy school very much during the winter. It's all right to like it in the fall while the football team is still winning, and it's all right to like it in the spring when FFA goes on a lot of field trips and you can wear short-sleeve shirts and roll the windows down on the pickup and look forward to summer. But nobody is supposed to like school in the winter, and nobody does. At that time of year, school is like winter itself—the worst part is dreading it.

But this year winter went better than usual, or at least faster. Almost before I had time to dread it, it had come and gone. Running every day gave me a reason to get through the day. I hated to admit it to just anyone, but I was having fun. Can you believe that? Running six miles a day in all kinds of weather, up and down the road to the cemetery and back, was fun. I liked the conversation with Chuck, and maybe I even liked myself better. I have discovered that if you want to be happy, you have to get along with yourself first, because you spend so much time with your own self.

Anyway, I woke up one day and it was Christmas already. And what a Christmas it was! Up till then we hadn't had rain at all, so everybody's wheat seed was just sort of lying in the ground trying to hang on until it could soak up enough water from somewhere to sprout and grow. When that happens, nobody in Wheatheart can be really happy. Oh, I was having a good year, with my running and all, but I wasn't really happy because no one else was. Even on the days when the dirt didn't blow and there wasn't any grit in the air, people acted like there was. When you are in high school, you really don't understand things like loans and interest and paying the bills, so you don't really know why people are so sad underneath. But you can understand the people enough to be sad with them.

But when I woke up on Christmas morning it was snowing. When I first woke up, I looked out my window like I always do, and there it was—snow! Big huge juicy flakes which splopped and splattered in big puddles when they hit. I just stood there for a long time and watched it come down. Even though it was Christmas, and we usually have a good time around the tree in the living room on Christmas morning, I still just stood there and watched the snow come down for a long time. God really gave us a nice present, and now everybody could be a little happier.

Chuck came over for dinner. His folks were going over to Alva to spend Christmas with old friends, people he didn't even know; so when I invited him to come to our house, I think he and his folks were glad. At our house, Christmas dinner is a little different, so that's the reason I was glad he came. We don't have turkey and dressing like they do on TV programs and in the movies. We have ham and black-eyed peas and cornbread and hominy. I am not sure I know why altogether, but it has something to do with memories. When my folks were growing up in Wheatheart, they were poor and that's what they ate on Christmas. If you ever had a happy Christmas when you were growing up, you seem to spend the rest of your life trying to have another one just like it. Like I said, I don't know why we eat those things on Christmas Day, but if it makes my mom and dad feel like Christmas, it's all right with me.

Chuck was especially good company that day, because he is not the kind of guy who goes around asking what you got for Christmas. At our house, we usually get one special gift and then the rest of the stuff is clothes, underwear and socks and things like that. Now, I am not ashamed of that, but I just never get too excited about telling anybody. In fact, I am glad for those clothes because one of the things you can do during Christmas vacation is clean out your sock and underwear drawers, move that old stuff to the rag drawer, and throw away all the old dirty car-waxing and shoe-polishing rags. I guess it is just one of those little things which make life worth living, particularly coming that close to New Year.

But before I leave Christmas, I need to tell you that my special gift was a new pair of Nike running shoes. I have no idea how my mom had any hint of what I wanted; I don't know how she figured out *where* to buy them, much less *what* to buy. But she did. When she gave me the box to unwrap, I could tell that she and my dad were pleased with what they gave me, so I was going to act pleased too, regardless of what it was. But when I got the box open and found those shoes, I really was happy and couldn't help showing it.

They were silver canvas with silver leather stripes running down each side. The soles were built out of little cleats which gave good traction and neat prints. As I tried them on, my mom was explaining something to me about how they were not like Chuck's because I had long skinny feet and these were shoes for people with long skinny feet. I guess that is what she said—I didn't listen. I was too busy looking and feeling and remembering way back to August when we ran that first day and I followed Chuck into the Whippet, admiring the way he ran and dreaming a wild dream that someday I might run like that.

Those shoes were the other reason why Chuck was good company Christmas day. I couldn't wait till our dinner settled enough for us to go run. By the time we drove down to the Whippet, it was about three o'clock. Although it had quit snowing a couple of hours before, we still had maybe four inches. Since the temperature was right about at freezing, most of the snow had stuck, except on the road where it had already melted into puddles. The wind wasn't blowing enough to wrinkle my shirt, and the whole world, or at least as much as I could see of it running up Cemetery Road, looked like a giant Christmas card.

Neither of us talked. We were too busy looking. I wish I could describe it better—it was worth being alive for. With my new shoes and all that snow lying so still across those open fields, I completely forgot about myself. My body just sort of melted away and became a part of my mind.

After a while, Chuck spoke, but softly, the way you would in church, "What's it like up at the foot of the hills?"

"You've never been there?" I shouldn't have asked. I should have known that he had never been there, but I sometimes forgot that he hadn't always lived in Wheatheart or been rabbit hunting and rock hunting, and just running around up on the river.

But he didn't make a big deal of my question. He just said, "Not yet."

My next question was just as natural as his answer. "Do you want to go?"

"Sure." He seemed excited abut it. "When?"

"Right now," was all I said.

We ran along for a long time, just looking again, and finally he said, "Okay."

So we went. We ran right past the one-mile road and the two-mile road and the cemetery and the old beat-up hay barn at the five-mile road, and we ran all the way to the foot of the hills where the road ends, exactly eight miles from the Whippet Drive-In. We talked a bit along the way, but we didn't have all that much to say. He bragged on my shoes a couple of times, and he got excited every time we flushed a covey of quail or a jackrabbit out of the weeds in the bar ditch. But other than that, we just ran, not really fast, but not slow either.

When we got to where the road ends, I asked him if he wanted to stop and explore for a while, but he said, "Nope. Sometimes you get into a situation where your brain just can't absorb all your eyes can see, and that's the way I am now. We'll just have to come back sometime."

On the way back, I began to feel my body some. It didn't hurt the way it did when I was out of shape and beginning to run, but it hurt in another way, almost like it was trying to remind me that I was in charge. A couple of times we stopped and ate some snow; but for the most part, we just kept on running, and we talked more. Now that our bodies hurt a bit, we needed more than scenery to pass the miles.

When we got back to the cemetery, I could feel Chuck beginning to slow down, and he said, "Osgood, you're going to have to run in by yourself."

"How come?" I asked like I didn't know.

"This is too far for me." He sounded weak and sincere.

"But you're the one who taught me how to do this," I reminded him.

"I know," he answered, "But today you have outdone your teacher."

"I'll quit too," I offered.

"No," he said. "You go on. You're still running too strong to quit now. I'll be all right. I'll walk for a while."

"Well, shoot. The only reason I wanted to run in was that I wanted to tell you a story." That wasn't true. I just made it up, but I had to say something.

"Osgood, I would run around the world just for one of your stories." He said it like he didn't mean it, so I looked over at him. He had his eyes crinkled.

Right then I couldn't think of a single story. Now, don't tell anybody I admitted that, because you lose your license to live in Wheatheart if you ever run out of stories. But I thought of one quick—something Brother Bob had told in church a couple of weeks before. Everybody in the crowd laughed, and Brother Bob acted like he thought it was funny, so I told Chuck, drawing it out as long as I could as we ran, but at a little slower pace.

"This new preacher went to this church, see. He was going to preach his first sermon. It was from over in Revelations. Have you ever read Revelations?" I waited for him to answer.

Finally, he just said, "No."

"Oh, well, over in Revelations somewhere Jesus says, 'Behold, I come quickly.' Now, that doesn't mean the first time, because He has already come the first time, so I think it must be when He comes again. You know about that, don't you?" and I waited for an answer.

"Not really."

"Well, it doesn't matter. That was his sermon, this new preacher. Well, when he got up to preach, he got really nervous. I know what he was going through. I get nervous in front of crowds too. Do you get nervous?" This time I didn't have to wait so long for an answer.

"Not usually."

"Well, this new preacher got so nervous he forgot his sermon. He couldn't remember one word of it. But he could remember his text, so he said that real loud, thinking something would come back to him. But it didn't. He still didn't know what to do, so he said the text again and pounded on the pulpit. Do you like preachers who pound on the pulpit?" This time I had to wait a long time for an answer.

"Never heard one."

"Well, if pounding helps the preacher, it's all right with me. But it didn't help this new preacher—he still didn't remember his sermon. So for the third time, he shouted 'Behold, I come quickly'," and pushed against the pulpit. Well, it slipped off the stage and the pulpit and the preacher both fell into the lap of a little old lady sitting in the front row. The preacher picked himself up and then picked her up and started to apologize. But she just said, 'Well, that's all right, Preacher, I should have known you were coming— you warned me three times.' ".

I waited for him to laugh or to say he hated it or something. Finally, he just said, "Stick to running, Osgood."

That story had taken me almost a mile to tell. I said, "If you think you're so funny, you tell me a story." So he did, something about a knight riding a St. Bernard out in a rainstorm. I really didn't get it, but that was all right, because it took nearly a half a mile.

After that, we sang Christmas carols. Now that was a scene to remember. The snow lay so still all along the fields; and the town itself looked like it was asleep in a white bed. By then it was nearly dark and the moon was beginning to peek through low gray clouds, just enough to give everything a glitter. We finished that sixteen-mile run singing Christmas carols, him with his deep voice singing in tune with the song and me with my squeak sometimes hitting the right note.

When we got back to the old Chevy and rested a bit, he said, "That's the last time you will ever have to carry me, Osgood."

I didn't know what he was talking about, so I just said, "I didn't notice you being all that heavy." He just crinkled his eyes. As I look back at it, I think this is the Christmas I will remember when I'm older and have my own kids.

16

The John Deere Place

The next day, I got a job, sort of by accident. I needed a job all right, but during that time of year, there just wasn't that much going on out on the farms, and that was the only kind of work I had ever done.

When I went down to the John Deere store to buy some brackets for the mirror on the old Chevy, Mr. Garland asked me if I would like to work there after school and on Saturdays. That was such good news that I suppose I shouldn't have asked for any favors, but I did. I told him I couldn't come right after school because I already have a daily chore for an hour or so. I was glad he didn't ask what. He just said that was okay, that I could come when I want to, and keep my own hours. I liked that idea so much I went to work right then—I didn't even go home for dinner.

I cleaned up the store, put parts away in the right bins, and put machinery together. With both running and working, the winter just flew by. Since we knew we could run sixteen miles, Chuck and I started doing all sorts of different things. Some days we would go ten miles, out to the old barn and back. Other days, we would race as fast as we could for half a mile and then jog the next half and race the next half. He almost always beat me in those half-mile races, but never by much. Once in a while, I would beat him, but I still didn't know whether he let me do that just so I wouldn't get tired of buying the cherry limeades. Although we always decided in the parking lot what we were going to do that day, it almost seemed at times as if he had thought about it before we got there.

Soon after I started working at the John Deere store, I discovered that it wasn't much like working on the farms. It was more social than anything else. During the winter there is always a crowd in the John Deere place or at the Dew Drop Cafe, and those people spend most of the winter catching up on what they might have missed during the busier seasons, and retelling the same stories they told last year but forgot they told.

Actually, there was more talk at the John Deere place than at the Cafe. Since they never had to stop to eat, they could cover a lot more ground. Usually, I didn't listen all that close since I really didn't make much sense out of it. The only time they talked about kids, it was football and Coach Rose or sometimes Mr. Benalli, but never anything really about kids themselves. They didn't care or they didn't remember what it was like to be a kid.

Once I was back behind the counter sorting different sizes and kinds of sickle sections and working at trying not to listen. Since it was cloudy and had been raining off and on all day, a big crowd had gathered. When the crowd got that big, the Garlands, Scotty's dad and grandad, would sit in their little offices made out of plastic walls, while the other people would gather around and sit on pop cases or hay twine sacks. Then stories really flew. It was kind of orderly with just one person talking at a time, but as soon as he finished, several others tried to jump in right at the period. I found myself picking out a favorite and kind of cheering for him to get in next. Right then, old Charlie Brady, Craig Brady's grandad, was telling some story about a bunch of steers getting drunk from eating corn silage. I had heard him tell the story before and I had read a similar story in one of those old farm magazines in Doc's office. I guess that kind of thing could have happened several places.

So while he was telling his story, I sorted fast and didn't listen much. All of a sudden, I heard my name. "Delbert, hey there, Delbert Ray." It was Lyman Jones who farms real big up by the river and runs cows all over the country. I looked over at him, and the whole crowd was staring at me.

"Yeah?" I said, and I wondered what story I would tell if it was my turn.

Mr. Jones, Lyman, went on. "Is that you I see out on Cemetery Road, running with that California kid?" When he asked it, everybody got really quiet and looked at me. I know people don't believe I can feel it when my face gets red, but I can, and I felt it then.

"Yes. Yes, Sir." You can thank my dad for that. Even though I had been working around for five years, I still called a lot of people Sir.

He acted interested. "How often you do that?"

"Every day." I started to say "Sir," but I didn't because I thought I almost heard everybody say, "Whew." At least it sounded to me like they wanted to. "Except Sundays," I added, but didn't say why. Those who cared would already know, and those who didn't care wouldn't understand anyway.

"How far?" He was doing all the asking.

"About six miles a day." Again I thought I heard everybody about to go "Whew," so I was going to tell them more, about Christmas Day and about the sixteen miles and about how it felt. I was ready and even thinking about it, but Mr. Jones interrupted again.

He said, "Well, keep it up, Delbert. That kind of thing can sure come in handy if you ever take up a career stealing watermelons." Everybody laughed as big as I ever heard them laugh, and long too.

The only reason they stopped is that Charlie Brady jumped in with "Or start makin' moonshine liquor." And they all laughed again.

Then somebody asked, "Well, who's going to quarterback next year?" And they quit laughing and got into a serious discussion again.

Right after that, I quit sorting sickle sections and went out to help the mechanics until closing time.

17

"This Town Is Slow"

I guess running wasn't enough for Chuck's winter. One day while we were out on a ten-mile slow run and talking a lot, he sighed big and said, "Boy, this town is slow in the winter."

"Yep." I agreed because I didn't know what else to say.

"So what do you do for excitement here all winter long?" He was impatient.

"We wait around until June and wheat harvest. Things really pick up then," I told him.

"I can hardly wait," he said, like he wasn't at all serious. "School's slow too. What do you do there?"

"We wait around until May and graduation," I told him again.

"I guess that is some consolation," he agreed with me. "At least, we're seniors. We are going to graduate. Think of that, Osgood. We're going to be high school graduates."

"Yep." I agreed because it sounded good to me."

"So what are you going to do after graduation?" he asked as if he really wanted to know.

"I don't know. I've never really thought about it." That was the truth. I had thought a lot about graduating and about being a graduate, but never about what I was going to do afterward. One nice thing about high school is that you don't have to ask what you are going to do. The next year you are going back to school to get one step closer to graduation. There's some comfort in that.

"You really haven't thought about it, Osgood?" He wasn't criticizing. He was just surprised.

"Nope." I wished we would change the subject.

"What about college?" he asked as if it was a possibility.

"I haven't really thought much about college." I decided to talk without his asking. "I'm not smart enough to be a doctor or a lawyer, and I don't like kids enough to be a teacher, and since I never played football, I won't get a scholarship, so I just never thought about college. Who knows? Maybe this job at John Deere will work into something for me." We ran along while both of us studied that answer. Then it was my time. "What about you?"

"Yeah," he said as if he had really thought it out. "I'm going to college all right. I am going to study advertising of some kind. I may work in print, but I really am thinking more about the electronic media, writing and production."

"It sounds like you are in a hurry to get there."

"Nope, I kind of like being a kid. You can do a lot of things you don't have to explain when you're this age. He sounded like he sighed when he answered.

"What do you mean?" I really wanted to know.

"Well, grown-ups have to have some reason for doing what they do or even for making a decision."

"Yeah." By then I saw what he meant. "You know what bothers me?"

"What?" He mocked me a bit.

"When some grown-up asks a kid, 'Why did you do that?' and the poor kid doesn't know what to say except, 'Because.' "

I wasn't really through, but he rushed in right then like some guys do down at the John Deere store. "That's it. I like being the age when 'Because' is a good enough answer." After that neither of us talked for a while, and then he said, "Let's make a deal. We just won't ever grow up."

Since I didn't understand that much, we didn't say anything for a while. Then he sighed again and said, "Boy, this place sure is slow during the winter."

"Well," I reminded him, "we do have the Jaycees Pancake Supper and Talent Show coming up."

"What?" He hadn't heard of it.

"The Jaycees put on this big pancake supper. It is supposed to be somewhere around February 2, so they can call it Ground Hog Supper, but since they can't ever seem to get everything put together at the right time, they just call it a pancake supper." I told him the whole history. He was learning more about Wheatheart all the time.

"So what do they do?" He was getting more interested, I think.

"Well, for one thing," I told him, almost bragging, "they serve *real* sausage."

"What's *real* sausage?"

"You know, in the casing," I reminded him.

"In what casing?" he asked like he had never heard of it, so I told him.

"The butcher packs the sausage in the intestine casings. It's really good that way."

"I'll take your word for it," is all he said, but a little later he asked, "What about the talent show?"

"Well, that goes with it. After the supper is over and we are all still in the gym, we have this talent show. Some good stuff."

"Yeah, like what?" He didn't sound like he was doubting me.

"Well, all the old fiddle players up north of the river come and fiddle. The trio from the Methodist Church sings a few numbers." I stopped and thought of some more. "Some of the kids from school play horns and piano and things like that. And the football team dresses up like a bunch of girl dancers. They stick balloons where they are supposed to have bumps."

"So this is really a big thing?" Since he asked again, I knew he was interested.

"Sure is. Maybe not as big as the high school graduation. That's the biggest thing of the year. And you don't dress up for this like graduation because of the pancakes and sausage, but almost everybody in town comes and has a good time."

"You've convinced me, Osgood, I now have something to live for." He said it like he had his eyes crinkled. "What about dates? Do people ever take dates to this pancake supper and clam bake?"

"Those who have girls do," I told him.

"Okay," he said kind of quick. "Let's go and take dates."

"Who?"

"Us," he said. "You and me. The Don Juan and the Lord Byron of Wheatheart."

Since I didn't know who those guys were, I forgot that part of it, and just said, "I'm not taking any date."

"Why not?" He asked like he was yelling at me. "Don't you like girls?"

"Sure I like them," I told him. "That's my problem. The girls I like, I like too much to ask them to go out with somebody like me."

He crinkled his eyes. "I wish you didn't think about yourself that way, Osgood, because I'm going to get a date. If you want to change your mind, just let me know."

"You go ahead," I told him. "I won't change my mind. Who are you going with?"

"Let's think about that," he said, like I was part of it too. "Who's the prettiest girl in school?"

If I had told the truth of my opinion, I would have said Connie Faye, but he didn't want the truth of my opinion. He wanted me to say what he thought so it would sound like he and I agreed. So I said, "Darla Sue Tucker."

He acted like he was thinking about that, but he wasn't. That is what he wanted me to say all the time. "You know, I believe you're right, Osgood. She *is* the prettiest girl in school."

"She's also head cheerleader and senior class secretary and she will probably play her saxophone in the talent show." I told him all that stuff as a warning.

He didn't act like he minded. "But does she have a steady date?"

"Nope," I assured him.

"Well," he said and he strutted like a band leader, "Darla Sue Tucker is about due for the biggest thrill of her life."

When he said that, I just ran off and sprinted all the way back to the Whippet, but it was only about half a mile.

18

The Nicest Boy in Wheatheart

The next day, without giving me much of a chance to vote on it, Chuck just decided that we were going to run half-mile races. That afternoon, we ran faster than we ever had before—Chuck really ran hard, and I just felt I had to follow. We ran those half miles just about as fast as I can run. Then when we got to the jogging parts, we were both so out of breath, we didn't say anything—just rested so we could run again. With all that running, I didn't get a chance to ask him how he came out with Darla Sue.

The day after that, he said we should run fast half-miles again, but after we started we were both too sore in the thighs for that, so we just jogged eight miles. When we got our muscles loosened up and our breathing right, I decided it was a good time to ask, so I did. I just blurted it out. "Did you ask Darla Sue?" I had a little tease in my voice, the way my dad used to have when he would ask me something about Connie Faye.

"Yep." He said it like he might not want to talk about it, but I wouldn't let him out like that.

"So what did she say?" I was still teasing a bit.

"She said a lot of things." He wasn't really telling me much.

"Such as?" and I waited a long time for an answer.

"She said I was the nicest looking boy in Wheatheart." He said that like he agreed with it.

"So is she going out with you?" I was beginning to feel good about it some.

"Not exactly." He was putting me off again.

"Why not? You got a bad reputation?" I wanted to laugh.

"Nope. She said I was about the nicest boy in Wheatheart too." He said it like he might have agreed with that too.

"So why isn't she going out with you?" I knew I didn't understand girls very much, but none of that made any sense at all.

"Because I don't play football." He stopped and thought. I didn't interrupt him or say anything. I just waited. When you know someone really close, you know when he isn't finished, and sometimes it's just best to wait for him without saying anything. When he got around to it, he told me the whole story. "Because I don't play that stinking game of football. That's it. Oh, she told me how nice I was, and how she really likes me, but she has her own reputation to think about. People just wouldn't understand her going out with someone who doesn't play football. It just doesn't seem right to all the guys who worked so hard for us to win the state championship." He said that last part like he was mocking her.

I wanted to tell him that I had warned him, but I didn't. He had already learned too much about Wheatheart. All the time, I was trying to think of something that would make him feel better, and me too. All I could think of sounded dumb and a little spiteful, but I said it anyway. "I hope her old saxophone won't blow in the talent show."

He didn't say anything. We just ran along and I had almost begun to think about something else. Then he said, "Why wouldn't it blow?"

"Something stuck in it?" I was just guessing at that point. I didn't know all that much about saxophones.

"Like what?" The way he asked, I could tell he was feeling better.

I thought about it for a while and said, "Paper." When he didn't say anything, I looked over at him. He looked back and crinkled his eyes and I said, "You wouldn't dare!"

He just said, "Wanna bet?" and started sprinting off. We raced the rest of the way in and I caught up with him at the north corner of the Whippet and beat him just because I could lean farther than he could. He just said, "I don't mind buying. Not now." So we sat on the tailgate of the old Chevy, dangling our feet and making plans.

19

The Tumbleweed Plot

Chuck went to the Pancake Supper and Talent Show with our family and we all sat together. We hadn't done that for years—I had always sat off somewhere with a bunch of the guys. It wasn't that I didn't like my family, but I always felt a little strange sitting with them at things like that. Not anymore. For some reason, I didn't mind sitting with them, and I didn't mind who saw me there either.

We always have this event at the high school gym because it is the only place in town big enough to handle that many people. The Jaycees cover the floor with tarps and set up big tables all around. First we sit and eat pancakes and real sausage. Then the Jaycees clear all the plates, which isn't any big deal because we use paper plates and plastic forks. After that we have the talent show up on the stage at the south end of the gym. Since the supper is one of those "All you can eat" deals, Chuck took seconds on sausage. At first, I didn't think he was going to eat at all; but after he tasted it, he took more.

While we were eating supper, Darla Sue came in and flitted all around the gym like a sparrow looking for grasshoppers. She never looked our way. She knew we were there, all right, but she never looked toward us. We were about the only people she missed. She flirted with every football player there, even the sophomores and some of the older looking freshman. She would pull their hair or take a bite off their plates or maybe even sit on their laps. She even kissed a couple on the cheek. They all liked it and so did the grown-ups around. They thought she was just being friendly, but I didn't.

After we had finished eating and were waiting around for the talent show to start, Chuck and I told my folks that we were going to the washroom. We left the gym and walked up to the north hall. We were just chattering along, talking about normal things so that people wouldn't suspect anything.

When we got to the bathroom, I asked Chuck if he had brought the paper. He just crinkled his eyes and unbuttoned his shirt. He had wrapped a whole roll of toilet paper around his body and had put his shirt over it. I guess if I had looked close enough, I could have seen he was a little fatter than usual; but since I hadn't noticed, I was sure no one else had.

We went out the bathroom door and sneaked down the west hall. Since that hall has a door opening right onto the stage of the gym, we figured the people in the talent show would put their stuff in one of those classrooms. Darla Sue would probably have her saxophone there, if we could just find the right room. So we went sneaking down the hall, slipping up and looking through those little slit windows in each room. We found the fiddle players in one, warming up and sawing away. In the next one we found the Methodist trio. They were just standing around talking to each other. But in the next room, we saw the saxophone case lying right there by the door. It was half open with the saxophone sticking out. That would have been perfect for our plot except for one thing—all the junior and senior football players were in there too, dressing for their big number as dancing girls. They had stripped down to gym shorts or bathing suits and were putting on makeup and panty hose and balloons and really being silly. When we saw them, Chuck and I slid down the wall and sat on the floor and just looked at each other. I think we both must have been thinking the same thing, because when I said, "Give me a few minutes, but you have to be quick," he just said back, "I am quick."

I sneaked out the hall and ran out to the football field. I knew exactly what I was looking for, because I had been seeing it from the FFA building for the past few weeks. There was a huge thistle, some folks call them tumbleweeds, stuck under the bleachers. I pulled it out; it was even healthier than I thought. After frost, these thistles die and turn hard and brittle. They have little stickers and big stems. I grabbed this one by the root which had been blown out of the ground back before Christmas when there wasn't any moisture. Then I started running as fast as I could down along the side of the building. I held that thistle out so it would rake across the windows and the screens as I ran by. Because it was so brittle, it made a horrible noise, almost worse than running a long piece of chalk up the blackboard wrong, I made sure I hit every room, including the one where the football players and the saxophone were. Then when I got to the place where the outside wall juts out a bit, I crawled into that little crevice and stood real still in the dark. I could see the shadows of the people running to the windows. I heard the windows open, and then voices, a lot of football players talking about what they thought they saw. Some saw a wild 'possum or coon running off toward the bus barn. Some thought a branch had fallen off one of the evergreens out by the grade school playground. Oh, they saw a lot of things, but they didn't see me. After all the betting and bragging had ended and they closed the windows, I sneaked around and into the north door, and walked slowly back to the bathroom. Chuck was waiting for me. He just crinkled his eyes, and said, "Let's work on your German again. You've got to get that gutteral sound way down in your throat but you cut if off quick. See, watch me," and we walked back down the hall with him teaching me to speak German words. I bumped into him once, making it look like an accident. The paper was gone.

We went back into the gym, sat down beside my mom and dad, and waited for the talent show to start. Jeff Devine who works down at the drugstore, and enjoys being Emcee more than other people do, told a few jokes and gave the order of the talent. Darla Sue was down about two thirds of the way through, so I had a long time to sit there and feel the palms of my hands get all sweaty inside. That's really bad at a talent show where you have to clap once in a while. But her time came. When she walked out on the stage, everybody clapped from just being polite. She told us what she was going to play; I forget the name, but it had blues in it somewhere. Then, just before she started, she winked really big. She didn't wink at anybody in particular—just everybody, and they all loved it. The whole crowd clapped and whistled again like she was the favorite. After Mrs. Meacham played a bit on the piano, Darla Sue put the saxophone up to her mouth and started to blow. Of course, nothing came out—not even a squeak. She just smiled at us and winked again. Mrs. Meacham played the same bit the second time, and again Darla Sue tried to blow with nothing coming out. This time she looked a little serious, and she fiddled with the mouthpiece some. Then Mrs. Meacham played the same bit again, and Darla Sue blew once more. This time, when nothing came out, the crowd just roared like they thought it was planned. Darla Sue looked at us with the strangest expression her face, like she was really scared, and she ran off the stage. By then the crowd was really laughing and clapping, but Darla Sue never came back.

I sat there feeling confused. I kind of wanted to laugh, but I really didn't want to either. I didn't know what to think of what we had done. What she had done to Chuck wasn't right. I knew that. And people shouldn't take themselves so seriously that they can't make a little mistake once in a while. But still, I couldn't help thinking how she must be feeling, and I really didn't want to make her feel that bad.

I looked over at Chuck thinking he would help me understand. He just sat there looking straight ahead, but he didn't have his eyes crinkled like I thought he would have.

Coach Rose's Hero

When I got to school the next day, I saw Darla Sue's dad was in the hall, chatting with Mr. Benalli. After a bit the two walked into Mr. Benalli's office and closed the door. The rest of the day one or two of the other guys, football players, were gone from every class. When the teacher asked where they were, somebody would say that they were in Mr. Benalli's office.

At lunch, Chuck and I sat off in a corner by ourselves like we had been doing ever since the football playoffs, but we were close enough to overhear some of the guys talking. They are always loud, but usually its because they want people to hear them. This day they were loud because they were mad. They all talked at once so it kind of ran together, but they said things like, "I know I didn't do it."

"Somebody did it and he had better admit it before we all get in trouble."

"I don't see how any of us could have done it."

"Yeah. Maybe somebody did it before she brought the horn down to the room."

"Not according to her. She played it after she got it in the room."

"Then it had to be one of us. Nobody else was in the room."

"If that guy doesn't tell soon, he is going to get his head bashed in. I can tell you that."

When the conversation got too fast and soft for us to hear, Chuck tried to teach me how to say "I am your friend" in Japanese, but I'm not very good with foreign languages.

About halfway through the last hour, the little freshman girl who picks up absence lists and runs notes for Mr. Benalli came into government class, walked over to my desk, handed me a note, and walked out again. It was one of those pink notes which come from the office and always look important whether they are or not. Everybody turned around and looked at me, including Mr. Harrison; so I just shoved the note aside like I was more interested in class than in that note. I must have acted pretty good, because he went on with whatever he was telling and everybody turned back to listening or whatever else they were doing. I opened the note. I didn't need to—I already knew what it said. In the words of a famous movie detective, "The jig is up." I just hoped we didn't get kicked out of school—or worse. The note said exactly what I thought it would say.

To:	Delbert
From:	Coach Rose
Topic:	If you have a few minutes, please stop by my room after school today. I would like to visit with you. CR.

The only surprise was that it was from Coach Rose. Benalli had been on the case all day. Why Rose now? That didn't make sense, but I still had to go. I was part of it and we had been caught. Now, I had to take whatever happened.

When the final bell rang, I put my books in the locker and started out to the shop class where Coach Rose taught and had his office. Chuck was waiting for me at the door like he knew I would be coming. I started to say something, but he interrupted me.

"Osgood, have I ever told you how to say, 'How are you?' in Chinese? Those people say, 'I hope you have eaten today,' " and that is what he talked about as we walked out to Coach Rose's office.

When we got there, Coach was working on something at his desk, but he put it away and asked us to sit down. Then he sat on the edge of the desk so he could be close to us. I tried looking at him, but I couldn't. But it wasn't because we were in trouble. I have always had a hard time looking straight at Coach Rose. It was like as if I was Moses trying to look at that burning bush. There are some things you just shouldn't stare at, and Coach Rose was one of those. I sneaked a glance at Chuck and he was looking straight at him, with his eyes crinkled even.

"I hear you boys have been running." That was how he started his speech.

I thought of the thistle and the windows and the footprints I must have made outside the windows, so I said, "I don't know what you mean, Sir."

He turned, looked at me and grinned, or I think he grinned, at least for him. "Running, Delbert. Out on Cemetery Road. You guys have been doing lots of running."

"That's right," Chuck told him. "We've been going every day."

"Except Sundays," I added. I don't know why I said that, but I thought it might come in handy a little later.

"That steady, eh?" Coach Rose put his hand under his chin as if he were thinking. "You ever run before?" he asked that of Chuck, because he knew about me.

"Yeah, some," Chuck said it like he didn't need to say Sir, but I wished he had. "In schools where I've been before."

"You guys very fast?" It sounded like Coach Rose was just being friendly.

"Nope." I was trying to be honest, but I was also trying to be humble. I didn't want him to think we were proud or anything. "We just lope along."

"That's not what I hear." He sounded as if he had good reports. "I hear you run fairly well. I just wanted you guys to know that I really admire you for what you are doing. Long distance runners—those guys are the real athletes in this world—they and gymnasts and ballet dancers." That didn't sound like it had come from Coach Rose, the man who had just run our undefeated football string to twenty-four games in a row, longest in the state. But he was standing there telling us that.

Chuck and I were both so surprised that neither of us could think of much to say except, "Thank you, Sir."

He wasn't through. I was afraid of that. "Guess who my hero was when I was your age?"

"Red Grange?" Red Grange was the only old football player I had ever heard about, and the only reason I knew of him was that he was on a little card in the sixth grade reading box. From the look on Coach Rose's face, I could tell it wasn't the right answer.

"Have you ever heard of Glenn Cunningham?" he asked us, like he was going to tell a story.

"No, Sir," we both said at the same time, like we wanted to hear it.

"Well, that's all I'm going to tell you," he said. "If you want to know more, you can look it up for yourselves." And now he really did grin. "Do you guys mind if I come out and watch you sometime?" he asked.

"No, Sir," I said.

"Any day after school," Chuck said, and we got up and left.

That day we ran the six miles out to the cemetery and back. We went out at a fair speed, but we raced back in, as fast as we could run the three miles. Chuck ran ahead most of the way, but I caught him about a hundred yards out from the Whippet, so we both sprinted as hard as we could the rest of the way. Right at the end, he got ahead by two steps and I just didn't have the stuff to get it back, so that is how we finished. When we got through panting and looked up, there was Coach Rose, sitting in the back of the old Chevy with his feet dangling out. He had been watching us all the way. He asked, kind of calm, "Do you guys drink cherry limeades?" We both answered as best we could, and he went and bought three jumbos.

Then we all sat in the back of the old Chevy dangling our feet while he told us about Jim Ryun and Roger Bannister and Bill Rodgers and Frank Shorter and Paavo Nurmi, and people like that. We listened, partly because he bought the limeades, but mostly because we liked stories, and liked him for telling them to us.

When we all got down to the slurping sound, he patted us both on the knee and said, "Like I told you, I admire you guys for what you are doing; and I am going to depend on you to do the right thing this spring." With that he got up and walked to his car; but as he left, I thought he still had more he wanted to say to us. That's what I thought, but I couldn't tell for sure.

21

Young Men's Fancies

The next morning, Chuck and I got out of study hall, went down to the library, and looked up Glenn Cunningham. He was a neat guy all right—being burned and still setting all those records. It was almost too much to believe. After we talked about it, we both understood why Coach Rose liked him so much, but we still didn't understand Coach Rose any better.

At noon we were over in the corner of the lunchroom eating, when about half of the senior football bunch came over to our table. As usual, Chuck was telling me something about Germany or France or Japan, and I was telling him about Wheatheart, so we didn't notice the guys until they were already seated. I worried about it some, but I looked at Chuck and he was calm, so I tried to be. They started eating, the way you think football players are supposed to eat, but they also wanted to talk to us—about running, of all things. Somewhere they had heard that we were running, and they wanted to know all about it.

"How did you get started?"

"How far do you go?"

"Do you run every day, even in the cold and the rain?"

"What are you going to do with it?"

"Does it hurt much?"

"How do you get your heart to beat like that?"

"How do you keep your legs from turning to jelly?"

Some of it was silly, but most of it was serious. At first, I let Chuck answer most of the questions, but he acted like he wished I would talk too, so I did.

I don't know whether they were impressed or not, but they said they could never do it, and they listened all lunch period without changing the subject.

After that, some of them started showing up once in a while down at the Whippet when we were finished, and we would sit around and talk and sip cherry limeades together. And before we knew it, spring came.

I like spring anytime. When the wheat gets big and thick and green and looks like it is going to make good, you try to remember how it looked when it was just seed; and you just shake your head and realize that there is a miracle going on. No need trying to explain. How those ugly beige seeds turn into those green plants is a miracle, and it reminds you that there is something happening in this world which is all right.

But I sure liked that spring. The old Chevy was running good. I was running good and because I was, I got to see more of the miracle of growing wheat than I had ever seen before—or at least I got to think about it more. Work was fine too—the Garlands were good to me and the crowd hadn't talked about running except that once. School was going good, and we weren't in trouble, at least yet. I didn't think much about Jimmy Charles any more, and when I did it was the good times we had had together and not about his being dead. And now the football players were drinking cherry limeades with me. I just didn't know what more I could want.

But Chuck did, and he brought it up. That's the way it is in life. About the time you get happy with what you have, someone tells you about something else you don't have, and then you are unhappy till you get it.

We were running the whole sixteen miles out to the hills and back that day, so we had a lot of time to talk. We also had a lot of time to look at the hills covered with trees of one green and grass of another green, and to notice how they stood out against the even deeper green of the growing wheat. For a couple of miles, I tried counting the different colors of green I could see from right there on Cemetery Road, but I kept losing track when I would stop to think about running or talk to Chuck. The hills are there forever and the talk was only for that day.

All at once, just as calm as he usually talks, Chuck said "We've got to get a date, Osgood. We've just got to get a date. I don't care what you think about girls; it's spring and spring is the time when young men's fancies turn to thoughts of girls."

I had heard that somewhere before, but didn't know where. I just said, "Yeah," like I wasn't interested.

"Where do guys take girls on dates here?"

Since his question didn't concern me directly, I didn't mind answering, "Steady or otherwise?"

"Otherwise. Guys like me and you."

"Well," I made the story longer than it needed bo be, but we were running sixteen miles. "Mostly they go over to Alva to a movie; then they stop and park and make out somewhere on the way home."

"What about steady?" he asked.

"Oh, they just mainly drag Main until midnight, then they go somewhere around here and park and make out." I was telling him as much as I knew, since I wasn't speaking from experience.

"That's not any good," he said, after he had thought about it. "That's just not good enough for two men of the world like me and you. We need to do something special." We ran along for awhile. I quit thinking about it and started looking at the hills again, but he said, really excited, "I've got it. By George, I've got it. There is a play over at the college at Alva next week. My cousin is in it. I'll get the tickets and you can pay for dinner."

"For who?" I asked like he was crazy.

"For you and me and our dates." He said that like I shouldn't ask again. Then he said, "Who are you going to ask?"

I knew what I was going to say right then, but I ran along for a long time not saying it, because I wanted it to look like I was still thinking about it. Finally, I said, "Connie Faye," and I sighed some, but only to myself.

"I was hoping you would say that. I like her. She's pretty too," and he said it like he wasn't making fun of me. The curiosity really built up in me with every step. When I couldn't wait any longer, I just blurted out, "Well?"

"Well, what?" he asked, like he didn't know he was supposed to talk.

"Who are you going to ask?" I almost yelled it.

He acted surprised that I asked. "Darla Sue. You said yourself that she is the prettiest girl in school."

22

Just Killing Time

The next day was one of the most exciting of my life for two reasons. I didn't sleep much the night before. I just stayed awake and tried to picture Connie Faye, and I rehearsed what I would say when I asked her. I practiced several different words, and when I came up with what I thought were the best ones, I practiced how to say them so I would sound sincere without being pushy.

That morning I got up early and could hardly wait till I got to school. I had decided that since I was going to ask her anyhow, I should do it first thing in the morning. That way I would get it over with, no matter what she said.

Well, when I got to school, I spotted her by her locker, so I went right over. People were in the halls, more than I would have liked, but I could talk soft, and anyway that was as much privacy as I was likely to get. She was really pretty standing there with her back half turned so I could see both her hair and part of her face at the same time. When I saw how pretty she was, I almost turned around and left. Who was I to think that a pretty girl like that would go out with a bean pole like me? I stood there in the hall, not going either way for a while, arguing with myself. She turned around and saw me, and yelled, "Delbert, you're just the person I've been looking for."

I thought, "This is going to be easy. Maybe she is going to ask me out." I went over to her, walking like a guy who has just bought a new car and paid cash.

She looked right into my eyes and said, "I am so happy to see you. My locker is stuck. I got my sweater caught in the thing and the door won't open. What can I do?"

That wasn't what I wanted her to say, but I didn't act disappointed, and I didn't act like I thought she was stupid for getting her sweater stuck. With my pocketknife, I took the screws out of the hinges, took the door off, unlocked it, and put everything back together. While I was doing that, we talked—but just to kill time. I told her that the wheat looked good and that I was running a lot and that I was really ready for graduation. She told me that she was baby-sitting a lot and that the peonies were blooming, and that she was really ready for graduation too. When I finished, she said, "It's so nice to have a man around when you need him." Then the bell rang and we both hurried to first-hour class.

I saw her again third hour, but we were having a test so we didn't get to talk. I did slip her a note. It said, "How is your poor sweater?"

She wrote back, "Holy." I thought that was funny.

I wanted to talk to her at noon, but the football players came over and sat with us again, so I didn't get to see her until school was out and she was in a hurry to catch her bus. I guess it is just as well, because by then I had forgotten the speech I had rehearsed. Maybe I had forgotten because I had lost confidence in it.

I just went up to her in the hall when there wasn't anybody around, and I said faster than I usually talk, and higher too, I think, "Chuck and I were thinking about going over to Alva to see a play a week from Friday night and we wondered if you would like to go."

"You mean a double date, Delbert?" She seemed interested enough.

"Who's Chuck asking?"

I said, "I'm not sure." I was pretty sure he wouldn't have the confidence to ask Darla Sue, even though he said he was going to.

"I'd love to go. Thanks for asking me." She said that like she really meant it, and then left to catch her bus.

I found Chuck and we went running. I could hardly wait until I found out, so I asked him as soon as we got away from the Whippet. "Did you ask her?"

"Of course," was all he said.

"Well, is she going?"

"Of course," he said again, and I never found out what happened.

Later as we got on down the road, he explained some important things about dates—things I guess I could have figured out for myself if I had thought about them, but still good stuff. He showed me how you point at something and then just let your hand slide back along hers. That way, you could hold her hand and make it look like it was an accident. He showed me how you stretch and just leave your arm up around her shoulders.

Then he asked, "Do you know how a bra works?"

I just laughed at first, but when I saw he was serious, I said, "Why do I need to know that?"

He acted a little surprised at my question. "Well, some of these days, when you have your hand around her, you may just want to reach down and undo her bra."

"I don't think I'll ever do that," I said.

"Why not?" he asked, like he thought I was strange.

"I just don't think girls like it." I didn't know that for sure, but I thought if I were a girl, I wouldn't like it.

"Sometimes you have to force your way with girls. That is just a part of the fun of dating, seeing how far you can get."

I said, "I don't see any fun in making her feel bad. It may be fun for you, but if it isn't for her, then it really isn't fun at all."

After that he didn't say anything for a long time, so I started running really hard, all the way back into the Whippet. I knew I was ahead of him, but I couldn't tell how far. He hollered at me, "Osgood, Osgood," and I slowed down, thinking he was hurt or something. But when I did, he caught up with me and said, "You're right." Then he sprinted off ahead of me again, beat me into the Whippet and made me buy.

23

Like Spring Wheat
Spring 1982

Getting ready for a date is harder work than going out on one, and maybe about as much fun. I had to borrow my folks' car, get my Sunday pants cleaned, shine my shoes, and ask off at work. And I had to think about it too. Maybe I didn't really have to think about it, but I did.

Every once in a while in class, I would catch myself looking at Connie Faye and thinking how pretty she was and how soft her hands were and how she was going to be with me one whole evening. I had a hard time trying to think what she would look like with me beside her, me with my long legs and big hands, and hair that flops all over my head. I just couldn't get my mind around that picture, so I tried thinking about school things for a while, but found I would rather think about Connie Faye. She was really friendly to me for the next week. She sat with me once in the lunchroom, she passed me a note in class, and she'd come over to talk to me in the hall. We didn't talk about dating—we just talked about school, weather, everyday things. In fact, I talked to her more that week than to anybody else except Chuck.

She also dressed really nice all week. I don't guess she went out and bought new clothes just for me, but it seemed like it. I had talked to her every day all year, but I had never really noticed that she had such nice clothes, soft and frilly things, until that week.

But I also saw Darla Sue a lot, and that wasn't very comfortable. She was really nice to me and friendly. She told me that she was happy about getting to go with us, but that didn't help me much. I would have felt better if she had been mad. Of course, she didn't know we had put the paper in her horn. I thought about telling her so she could get mad and cry and maybe hit me; then it would be over and I could feel more comfortable. But I was too afraid to tell her, so I just went on looking forward to the next Friday, but dreading it at the same time.

Finally Friday came. We picked up the girls and drove to Alva. They were both really pretty that night, but in a different kind of way. Darla Sue was pretty like the hills up along the river when we ran. You could just look and look at her and never get tired of it; but even with all the looking, you knew you were never going to run all the way up there; you would always be here and they would always be there. But Connie Faye was pretty like a field of spring wheat, growing green, really pretty, but something you could wade through and feel around you, something you could stand out in and be a part of.

When we got Alva, we ate supper at a real restaurant, not like the Dew Drop at all; and as we left, I put two dollars on the table. I felt Chuck looking at me, so I turned and saw him crinkling his eyes.

Then we went to the college to watch the play. It was a musical called *My Fair Lady*, with singing and dancing. It was about this girl just off the street who was really rough around the edges. This professor took her into his home and made a sophisticated lady out of her. I guess that would be possible, but it seems to me there has to be something in the person that wants to change in the first place. During the play, I glanced over at Chuck and Darla Sue once in a while. He had put his hand up around her shoulders. It looked so natural for him to do it that I thought I might try that with Connie Faye, but then my whole arm felt like it weighed a hundred pounds, so I decided not to try it.

The only thing that really bothered me about the play was the band—or orchestra, they called it. We sat close to it and could watch this guy play his saxophone. Everytime he did, I thought about Darla Sue, and I sweated more than I should have.

As we drove back to Wheatheart, Connie Faye acted like she wanted to sit in the middle of the seat closer to me, but we all four started looking at the stars out the car windows so she slid over by her window to look better. On the other hand, Darla Sue and Chuck looked out the same window and got real close to each other. Usually, I like to drive, but that night I wished I hadn't.

When we got back into Wheatheart, someone said that we ought to stop the car so we could look at the stars really good, with it being such a calm and pretty night. So we drove up to Jaycee Park. It isn't all that much of a park, but it can be a nice place to be sometimes. It has a croquet court where some of the old-timers come to play when it isn't too hot or too cold, and it has some swings and a merry-go-round, and some trees and grass. About the time we got there, Earl Bresserman drove by, shined his spot light on us, saw who we were, honked like he was trying to be friendly, and drove on.

We swang some. Chuck and I pushed the girls and then they pushed us. Swinging was good because it gave us a chance to see the stars. We rode the merry-go-round, but slow so we wouldn't get dizzy. We might have been acting like kids, but we were at least acting like grown-up kids. After that, Connie Faye and I took a walk, up the street, around Doc's house, and back down. When we got out away from the lights of the park, I thought she might not see a crack in the sidewalk, so I just automatically took her hand to help her across. I really didn't even think about it much and I hadn't planned it, but all of a sudden I was just walking along holding her hand. She held mine back too, so we walked along in the dark under the stars, holding hands, and talking really easy, about things like going to school and growing up. I felt different than I have ever felt before in my life.

When we got back to the park, Chuck and Darla Sue were sitting in the swings, just rocking back and forth. They told us to go on home, that they would walk, so I took Connie Faye to her house. I had heard about guys walking girls to the door, but I didn't know how to do it. Did I need to say something to her or should I just jump out of the car and run around and open the door? It seemed that whatever I did, it wouldn't look like the right thing anyhow. So I just did it. I went around to her door, opened it, let her out, and walked with her all the way up on the porch. I guess in some places, that would be the man's thing to do because she might get attacked on the way. But in Wheatheart the only guy who would attack her would be the one walking her to the door.

At the door, Connie Faye was quick, and I was glad for that. I had about run out of nice things to say without making something up and sounding really silly. She just said, "I had a really nice time. Thanks for asking me." We stood there and looked at each other and then we kissed. I don't know whose idea it was. It just seemed to be something we both wanted to do but were almost afraid to. That was the first time I had ever kissed anybody on the mouth and I was surprised how everything fit. Sometimes even yet when I look at Connie Faye and see how her mouth and nose are, and how mine are, I still don't understand how it all fits when we kiss, but I am glad it does.

That night I didn't sleep too good, but it wasn't for the same reasons I hadn't slept good some other nights that year. When I woke up in the middle of the night, I didn't have tears in my eyes from remembering things that had happened earlier in the year, but I still felt special—in a happy sort of way.

24

Part of the Crowd

Chuck and I ran early the next morning, what with it being Saturday and my having to go to work. We both felt good, so we had a good run and an even better talk. Chuck asked me a lot of questions about what Connie Faye and I had done; I told him some, but not very much. There are just some things which happen only to you and you don't tell anybody, not even the guy you run with.

Then it was my turn. Remembering some of the instructions he had given me, I wondered if he had tried any of that with Darla Sue. I hoped he hadn't. So I asked, "What did you and Darla Sue do?"

"We talked." He wasn't going to tell me much either. After I thought about it I was kind of glad he was that kind of guy.

But I still asked, "What about?"

"I told her I put the paper in her horn." He just said it as we ran along.

I tried to think about what must have happened after that. I would have bet she hit him, and that she cried. Then I tried to think about how it was going to be all over town by the time we got back to the Whippet, and I didn't like that thought. I was glad she knew, but I just hated to go through what we now had to, because she knew. I guessed her dad was still mad. After thinking about it as long as I could by myself without needing some help, I asked, "What did she say?" I tried to sound as calm as he had.

"She said she already knew."

"How?" I was surprised, but scared too, so my voice was really high.

"She just figured it out." He was still calm.

"All by herself?" I still couldn't believe it. I thought he was making it up.

"All by herself."

"How?" I was still a bit scared.

"She said that after she had quieted down enough to think about it, she realized that the trick was too different for one of those regular guys; so she asked herself who would be mad enough at her to do something like that. And she came up with me."

I admired the way her mind worked. I guess when you thought about it, we had to be the logical ones; but I doubted that anybody else in town had thought that much about it, except maybe Coach Rose. "So how come she went out with you?" I asked, because I still wasn't sure I understood.

He went on as calm as he always was. "She said she was really mad at me for a while, even hated me. She cried herself to sleep at night and tried to think of ways to get even. But then she realized that she had been wrong in the first place. She had hurt me for no reason. She said she realized how silly she had acted about the whole thing, and that she probably had it coming. So after a while, she quit hating me and started liking me, even more now than she had hated me before."

"What else did she say?" I knew that was a dumb thing to say, but I wanted to hear more and didn't know how to ask.

"She thanked us for teaching her a lesson, and she laughed about how she must have looked up there that night on stage."

"She didn't hit you and scream and cry?" I still was having a hard time believing it.

"Nope, she just thanked us."

Now, I didn't know how to feel. I would have felt better if she had hit him and screamed at both of us. She owed us that. We had treated her wrong, and I wouldn't feel good about it until she got mad back. I appreciated her for being so grown-up about the way she felt and acted, but I didn't like me very much for what I had done.

When we got back to the Whippet, some of the senior football players were there, sipping cherry limeades and bragging about what they were going to do with their dates or the girls they picked up that night. Since none of it sounded like what a real date was like, I didn't tell them what we had done the night before. As they were about to drive off, they backed up and yelled out the window, "You guys don't forget to come to the April Fool's thing." Then they drove off.

Chuck turned around and looked at me. "What's the April Fool's thing?" he asked, like he was mocking a football player.

"It's something the senior boys do every year. Even though nobody gets to go except seniors, they pass it on year by year because they tell other people to keep it up. They go out to Wagner's Pond late at night—at least, those who drink beer do—and they all go skinny-dipping."

"Isn't it pretty cold?" Chuck seemed to be making fun of them.

"Maybe not if you drink enough beer." I told him, but I didn't know.

"Why did they invite us?"

"I don't know, now maybe we're part of the crowd."

"Oh, I hope not," he crinkled his eyes as he said it. "But it does sound like fun."

"You mean you want to go?" I was a little surprised, but maybe not. I would have felt bad if they hadn't asked, but I still didn't want to go.

"We'll see," he said. I went on to work, putting together machinery and thinking more about other things than what I was doing.

25

The April Fool's Thing

Those football players mentioned the April Fool's thing several more times, and they always included Chuck and me like we were going to be there. I still didn't know. I would go if Chuck did, though I didn't really want to—I wouldn't feel right being there. I wasn't going to drink beer, so that didn't bother me. No matter what anybody said, I didn't have to drink beer.

It was good, though, to be in on the event. This was a big deal for the football players. They had plans to make so they talked a lot, but they also tried to keep everything a secret. Sometimes it seemed that talking about it was more important than keeping it a secret, and by the time April Fool's Day came, everybody in town knew more about the party than the planners themselves. I guess it would have been easier if they had put up a big banner which said, "April Fool's Thing Tonight." The way it was, they thought they had a secret from the grown-ups, and that was important to them.

Weatherwise, April is no joke. The weatherman was good to us, really good, which isn't always the case this time of year. It was still a little too early for those boiling purple clouds filled with hail and tornadoes, which can sweep across the prairie and scare the dickens out of everybody and destroy all the wheat in a matter of minutes.

But we could still get some powerful winds that time of year—winds that whip across all the green fields and pick up just enough dirt to make life in general nasty.

But that year, April Fool's Day was beautiful and Chuck and I went out for a long run. On a really pretty day in the spring, when the wind blows just enough to rustle the growing wheat, the sky seems a million miles high—like a big, soft blanket from one corner of the earth to the other, rich blue with just enough white puffy clouds to make you want to look at it forever. If you ever come to Wheatheart, I hope you see the sky on a pretty day. It isn't one of the things we brag about, like the elevators or the banks or even the football team, but it is something which makes the place kind of special. Maybe we ought to advertise for tourists—"For the thrill of your life, come to Wheatheart on a clear day to see the blue sky." But, if a lot of people came, they would make noise and that would change what our sky is all about in the first place, quiet and peaceful.

Running with Chuck that day was quiet and peaceful. At times, I felt like I wasn't just running *under* that big blanket of a sky, but actually running *through* it, bouncing from one white cloud to the next. And the wheat smelled just like the sky looked, quiet and peaceful.

Chuck came to our house for supper; and after we ate, he and I helped my mom with the dishes. I don't know why we did that for sure, but it seemed like something we wanted to do the night of the big April Fool's thing. My mom didn't mind either, except when Chuck acted like he was going to wash and she shooed him away.

We didn't get specifically on any subject, but all three of us knew what we were talking about, even though we tried to act like we didn't. We asked my mom to tell us about the pranks they used to pull when she was a kid. Well, that question always gets my folks to talking. Even if they start with, "I didn't do any of this, but some of the kids did," they always get around to saying, "When we were kids we didn't have the money to run around in cars like you kids do, so we had to make our own fun." I don't know what that means for sure, but they say it.

She told us about the time they put a sheep in the English room, and when they tied Mr. Casteel's car to a tree and about stealing watermelons, and putting molasses on Mr. Baker's car door handles—things like that.

Chuck asked her why she thought kids pulled pranks. She told him that she didn't know for sure. It was just what kids were supposed to do. But all the time, she had that look in her eyes that told us there was more to her answer than what she had said.

Through the whole conversation, we never talked about the April Fool's thing. We just acted like she wouldn't know anything about it, but I know she did. They probably had it when she was a kid; but even if they didn't, she and her friends would have talked about it on the phone and in the store. She knew when it was and what was going to happen, but she just didn't say anything. She didn't tell me I couldn't go or give me any advice about how to act if I did.

I think deep down inside, she wished I wouldn't go; but I think she also knew that she couldn't tell me that, because I might go anyway. So she just acted like she didn't know anything was going to happen. I guess that is just one of the sacrifices parents have to make—they have to let loose of their kids even when they don't want them to do some things. And parents also have to act dumber than they really are.

After the dishes, Chuck and I drove the old Chevy for a while, waiting till it got dark. Then we headed out toward Wagner's Pond, about ten miles southeast of town. The pond is in Mr. Wagner's pasture, with grass and trees around, and it stays deep all the time, even in the dry years. It is a good place for duck-hunting, and sometimes couples go there to make out. And once a year the senior boys have a party and skinny-dip.

When we got about a mile away and started up the dirt road toward the pasture, Chuck said, "Let's jog the rest of the way." I didn't know why he wanted to do that, but it sounded like a good plan to me. We parked the old Chevy in a field behind a fence row, so nobody could see it from the road, and we jogged kind of easy over the hills to Wagner's Pond. When we got up on the closest hill more than a quarter of a mile away, we sat down in the grass where none of the guys could see us, and watched them.

By then, they were already pretty loud, cussing and bragging. Even those who weren't drinking were loud. Once in a while they would push each other and act like football players are supposed to. I figured they were trying to get up enough nerve to skinny-dip, what with the temperature down about sixty.

Chuck and I just sat on the hill and watched it all and talked. "Did you ever drink beer?" He asked like it was all right to ask me things you might not say to just anybody.

"Nope. I've tasted it, and best as I can tell, it tastes like canned chicken noodle soup before you pour the water in."

A few minutes later, he asked, "Why not?"

I thought about it for a while—not why I don't drink beer but how I could tell him. Then I just said, "For the same reason I don't run on Sundays."

We sat for a while more and watched the guys down at the pond. I asked, "What about you?"

"Nope."

"Why not?" I really wanted to know.

"Just never saw any reason for it." He talked calm. "I was afraid I would get drunk and then something funny would happen and I would be too drunk to laugh."

I looked up at the stars and tried to name those Chuck had taught me. I held up my hand and let the wind blow against it. After doing that for a while, I said, "I like my reason better."

He just said, "I think I do too."

Then we sat and watched as the football players got louder and bolder and dared each other, until finally they all took off their clothes and jumped into Wagner's Pond. They yelled and swore and laughed for a long time, but none of them came out.

Chuck said to me, "Do you think they are having fun?"

"Not as much as we are," I said, and we watched some more. Chuck then said, kind of calm, "How quiet can you run?"

I said, "Quiet enough." Then we got up, bent over low and

jogged real quiet down to the edge of the pond where the clothes were. We worked quick and careful. We dumped out billfolds and belts but still took a lot of stuff—pants and shirts and underwear and socks. That way some guys didn't lose but maybe one thing, but some guys lost everything.

Then we bent over low and jogged back up the hill. When we were out of sight, we really ran to the old Chevy. By the time we got there, I was laughing so hard I could hardly see. Chuck just crinkled his eyes.

We dumped those clothes in the back of the pickup and took off. I still didn't know what we were going to do with them, but Chuck said, "To the arena, Jiggs," in his best English accent. We drove around to the west side of town, staying on back streets to avoid Earl Bresserman, then went back up Half Mile road behind the football field. We parked and carried all the clothes right to the middle of the Whippet Football Field, where we made a really neat design with them on the grass. We scattered the colors around and put everything in patterns so it all looked like a giant flag from the west end zone.

I was kind proud of it when we were finished. Then we went home and I slept well that night.

The next day, all the senior football players came to school looking bleary-eyed and a little sad, and they had new nicknames for each other—like One Sock and No Shirt and Stripped Down and so on.

At noon, they all came over to sit at our table for lunch but before they could say much, Coach Rose came over walking like he wasn't going anywhere in particular, and said to me and Chuck, "Well, I hear you guys have been doing the right things this spring, like you promised me." I thought he was talking about our running, but I didn't know for sure.

After he left, Chuck and I told the guys we were sorry we missed the party but we couldn't go because we didn't want to mess up our running. When we asked them if they had a good time, they told us all about it, except for the clothes part.

26

The Time To Go Public

Since I had already done it once, I decided it would be easier to ask Connie Faye out for a date the next time, and it was. We went out quite a lot that spring. Sometimes we would go with Chuck and Darla Sue, and sometimes we would go just by ourselves. But we always tried to do different things. We played in the park a lot. We went walking around town, and that was really different. Nobody in Wheatheart ever walks, except for the widows who don't know how to drive or have lost their licenses. We rode bicycles. We went out to the Reinschimdt Farm and rode a horse one afternoon. We even bought wieners and went out to Wagner's Pond and cooked them. But we never parked and made out. That way, when we did kiss, it was nicer than it would have been if we had been doing it all the time.

The Sunday after April Fool's Day, Chuck came to church, all by himself, and he has been coming ever since. I don't know what made him do it. I was just sitting in Sunday School thinking about things and he said, "Slide over, Osgood." So I slid over and there he was. After that, we always sat together. I did say once, "I'm glad you're coming to church."

He said, "So am I," and that was that.

He was there for Easter and heard the sermons about how Christ had to die, and how He was planted in the grave and then rose in all His glory. That morning Brother Bob said, "It's like spring wheat. You sow those seeds in the fall. They give themselves up so we can have glorious growth." And I thought of our seed-cleaning days and our first days at running and some other things that happened in the fall.

Running just got better all the time. By Easter, we could race all the way out to the cemetery and back. Chuck beat me most of the time, but he had to work hard to do it. Sometimes I wasn't sure whether I followed him because he was faster or because I was supposed to.

The Monday after Easter, when we all went back to school and started counting days until graduation, a girl from Mr. Benalli's office came into second hour study hall and handed Mrs. Bell a note. She just barely looked up from her paper grading and said, "Charles and Delbert Ray, report to the office." She is the only teacher who calls me Delbert Ray and that's because she taught my folks. By calling me Delbert Ray, she makes me sound like a little kid and she doesn't have to think about how old she is.

We followed the girl back to the office. We tried to get her to tell us what it was all about, but she wouldn't say. She acted like she didn't know. Sometimes the best way to keep your mouth shut, when you are supposed to, is to act stupid.

When we got into the office, Mr. Benalli was seated behind the desk; Coach Rose was looking relaxed in one of the chairs, and Mr. Casteel was walking around the room. Chuck and I sat in the other two chairs, but not as easy as Rose was.

Since it was Mr. Benalli's office, he acted as if he was supposed to do all the talking, but he also acted as if he needed Casteel's permission to say anything. I felt sorry for him.

"Coach Rose tells us that you fellows have been active this year." He said it friendly enough, I guess, but I didn't hear it all that friendly. I thought of the jersey on the flagpole and the perfume in the football pads and the paper in the horn and the clothes on the football field, and my heart beat louder and louder. I put my hands on my knees because they needed a place to be and my knees needed something to hold them down. I tried to look up at the men, but I couldn't see all of them and I didn't know which to look at first. So I looked at Chuck. I couldn't believe he had his eyes crinkled.

Mr. Benalli went on. "We think the time has come for you to go public with all that effort."

I might have cried, except I knew it wasn't the right thing to do.

Like he was king or something, Casteel said, "Well, I'm not convinced."

Now, I was not only scared—I was confused. I didn't know what they were expecting from us. Then Coach Rose spoke. I think he knew I was scared because he looked at me, and it seemed almost as if he had his eyes crinkled too. "I told these men about your running. Frankly, I think you are good enough to run in a track meet—and see what all this effort you have put out is worth."

I breathed again, but I couldn't feel my heart. When I looked over at Chuck, he was just sitting there with his eyes crinkled.

Mr. Benalli explained some more. "This year for the first time in Oklahoma, there is going to be a 5,000-meter race in the district and state track meets. Do you know how far 5,000 meters is?" I could have figured it out if they had given me time. We had that stuff in math earlier in the year, but Chuck beat me to it. He said, "A little over three miles. Twelve laps and change around a quarter-mile track." And I thought to myself, "Out to the cemetery."

"Can you guys handle that?" Casteel asked like he thought we couldn't.

"We have trained," Chuck told him. "I don't know how fast they run in this state, but we can keep a strong pace for that distance."

"I've seen them run," Coach Rose broke in, "They can run that far."

Mr. Benalli got the floor back. "We're thinking of letting you guys go over to the district track meet in Alva. We haven't run track in several years here. We've been too busy with football—and sometimes basketball," and then he laughed just a bit, like that was supposed to be funny. "What do you think?"

"Well, I'm against it." Casteel spoke for us. "We've got a good school here, a good athletic program. Everybody knows us for quality, and I don't want to mess that up. No siree. We've worked too hard to get it this way. I don't want you guys to go over there and embarrass us. Besides, we've got enough for these kids to do with football and basketball. Put in track and first thing you know you're overemphasizing sports in a school. And I won't let that happen, not here. Not over my dead body!"

Chuck said, "We would be honored to represent Wheatheart at the district track meet, Sir. Thank you for putting your trust in us. We won't let you down." I don't know what got into him. I had never heard him talk to any adult like that. I think Casteel actually smiled. At least, there was a funny look on his face which I had never seen before. Then he said, "Well, we'll see. Coach, you'll be responsible for this."

Coach Rose said, "Yes, Sir." With that Casteel left and the four of us sat around looking at each other. Coach Rose said again, "Come on, I'll walk you back to class." When we got out the door, he asked us, "What did you find out about Glenn Cunningham?" So we walked down the hall telling him.

When we got to the door of the study hall, we stood outside in the hall and he said, "I'll enter you guys in the meet, and I'll take you to Alva a week from Saturday. But I'm not going to coach you. Not now. After all the work you've done on your own, it would be unfair to you for me to try to move in on whatever achievement you might win. No. I'll enter you and I'll take you, but you just keep training on your own. You know more about running than I do anyway." With that, he walked down the hall.

27

A New State Record

We spent the next two weeks getting our legs in shape for the district race at Alva. I had even more work to do, since I had to get my head in shape. I guess I should have been happy we were going to race, and I was, in one way. But in other ways, I wasn't as happy as I could have been. I thought all this time we had been running because we liked it, and liked each other. But now, by running in this race, we would start doing it on purpose and it wouldn't be fun anymore. Chuck told me that wouldn't happen. We would run like we always did, with the race just thrown in. I asked him how he knew and he said he had run races before. But he didn't say how many or anything.

Also I didn't want to run in front of all those people. Like I told you before, I turn red sometimes, and I knew I would in a race. Racing is not like football. In a football game, you are out there with a bunch of other guys doing about the same thing, so you can think you are lost in a crowd. But in a race, you are out there all by yourself. Chuck said that didn't matter because nobody watched you anyhow, not in a 5,000-meter race, at least. Even if there was a crowd and there usually wasn't, everybody would go get a hotdog during our race, so there wouldn't be anybody watching us.

I was also bothered about what Casteel had said. I know Casteel goes on a lot, but mostly he speaks for the town. He has been here long enough that he can do that. He knows what they think; and if they don't think it yet, they will after he says it. He said we might embarrass the town and ourselves. I didn't want to do that. This was my hometown and I didn't want to do anything to hurt it. Chuck said that didn't matter because we were fast enough that we wouldn't embarrass anybody. I didn't know how he knew that, but I had to take his word for it because I didn't have anything better to believe.

As you can tell, we did a lot of running those next two weeks, and a lot of talking too. On Thursday, the last day we ran before the race, I noticed how much the wheat had grown since the last time I looked, and it bothered me some that I had been too busy to notice. In other years. I wouldn't have really noticed because I didn't know enough to care. But this year when I had finally learned to care, I let myself get too occupied to notice before.

Saturday came and Coach Rose took us over to Alva. He kidded us about checking out a bus for his track team, but he decided to use his own car instead. When we got there, I was sure surprised. I thought a track meet would be something like a football game, but it wasn't. It was more like a circus. At a football game, there is just one thing going on for the crowd to look at. At a track meet, everything is going on at the same time. Some guys are running, and you have to stay out of their way. Some guys are jumping and you have to stay out of their way; and some guys are throwing things and you really have to stay out of their way. But mostly, a whole bunch of guys are just lying around out in the middle waiting for their turn to run or jump or throw. While they're waiting, they act as if they're on a picnic or something—throwing frisbees and just relaxing.

Chuck knew what to do, so I followed him out in the middle of the field. He hunted for the right spot, reminding me of an old cow looking for the right place to lie down; then we just relaxed and waited. I didn't relax much though, since I wanted to watch the other guys run. They all seemed so fast, and knew what they were doing; and they dressed like it was important. They had on silly-looking thin shorts and shirts and real track shoes. A lot of them didn't even wear socks, and I thought that was strange.

On the way over that morning, Coach Rose had handed us both some old basketball trunks, green with white stripes, and he told us we could wear our white T-shirts so we would be in Wheatheart colors. Then he gave each of us a brand new pair of real gym socks. I thought I would really look like a runner when I got all that stuff on; but when I got to the track meet and found those guys not wearing socks, I didn't know what to think. Chuck's green and white Nike running suit actually looked better than what Coach Rose had given us, and I thought he might wear that since it had the right colors. But he didn't.

After we had waited most of the afternoon while the other guys ran the short races, the man on the loudspeaker said, "First call for the 5,000 meter." When he said that, Chuck and I got up, stripped, stretched, and walked over to the starter. When I stepped on that track, I could tell it was going to be nice running. It looked like the asphalt on Cemetery Road, but it wasn't. It was really soft, like it had some rubber in it.

A whole bunch of guys showed up to run. They were all dressed like real runners and they looked very serious. I was scared, and thought about just walking off the track. Maybe I could tell Coach Rose I had a stomachache, which wouldn't have been that much of a lie. But then, I started looking at each one till I found this one guy, short and kind of chunky, and I said to myself, "I can beat him." I lined up right next to him at the starting place, and when the man fired the gun, I just ran beside this guy I picked out to beat. I stayed right with him all the way around the first curve. By then, nearly everybody was ahead of us, but I still knew I could beat this guy if I stuck with him. But when we got around that curve, we just weren't running as fast as I normally did, so I went out into an outside lane and passed most of the bunch. When I got up near the guys in the front, I spotted Chuck already out in the lead a ways, so I ran up and got in behind him. He and I just ran that way all the way around, with him out front and me about three yards behind. When we got back around to where we had started, some guy held a big sign with an 11 on it. At first, I didn't know what it meant, but then I figured it was the number of times we still had to run around the track.

Chuck and I ran the next lap together like that, with my staying about three yards behind. I might have caught up and run beside him for aways like we usually did, but those curves made it longer, so I just stayed behind. He knew I was there, so it was almost like being out on Cemetery Road, except the scenery wasn't as nice. I tried looking around some, but there wasn't that much to see, just people and a football field out in the middle. So I quit trying to see much and just ran and thought and enjoyed myself. I got so involved I even forgot to pay much attention to the man holding the signs, telling how far we still had to go. I also forgot to worry about when the really fast guys were going to pass us. I knew we were ahead, but I knew before we got in, someone else would probably take over. Oh, I knew when we had to go out of our lane and pass guys sometimes, but those were the slow ones. In fact, I remembered passing that little chunky kid at least twice and maybe three times. But about the time I was getting really comfortable with running, and had forgotten to be embarrassed with all the people looking, we ran by the man with the gun and he shot it, right in Chuck's ear. Well, Chuck took off running as fast as he could, like he thought the man was shooting at him. I didn't know for sure what the shot meant, but I took off too. Chuck is faster than I am, so when we run full speed he can almost always beat me, and that day he did gain on me some. By the time we came back around and had passed a lot of other guys, Chuck was maybe ten or fifteen yards ahead of me. Just before he got to the finish line, somebody pulled a little string across the inside lane and Chuck broke it when he went through. I ran in just behind him; some man who looked official said, "This is second place," and I realized then that we had won.

We had won! The race was over and we had won. I didn't know the right thing to do. I thought about jumping up and down like I was happy, and I thought about running and hugging Chuck like I had seen guys do on television, but all that didn't seem right. So I just walked up to him and grinned. He said, "You're all right, Osgood," and he crinkled his eyes. Then we walked around the outside of the track really slow and talked about how it felt, about passing everybody and about running around and around in circles without going anywhere and about it being through before we knew it was over. Coach Rose caught up with us and gave us each a can of pop. It wasn't as good as a cherry limeade, but it was all right. I could tell he was happy, happier, I think than I had ever seen him, even after a football game.

When everybody had finished the race, the man on the loudspeaker said, "Ladies and Gentlemen. First place in the 5,000 meter is Chuck Murphy of Wheatheart. Chuck's time was 13 minutes, 34 seconds. According to the records we have now, that is a new state record, a new state record by 7 seconds. And it is 21 seconds off of the national record of 13 minutes and 13 seconds. In second place is Delbert Goforth, also of Wheatheart. Those Wheatheart boys must chase a lot of jackrabbits." He said that last part like he meant it to be funny, and some people laughed. Then he went on with third and fourth, but I didn't hear the rest. I was too excited. We had won; but more than that, we had set a state record. We were the best in the whole state! At least, Chuck was. I couldn't believe it.

When the crowd quieted down to watch another race, we all went over and stood on this box with different levels. Chuck stood on the highest level, of course, but I stood on the second highest, and the officials came by and hung these huge medals around our necks. I have tried to remember how I felt right then, because I had never felt that way in my life before, and may never again. But that doesn't matter. I did once, and that makes me luckier than most people, I guess. It would be great if everybody could just once feel like I did when the official hung that ribbon around my neck. Just once would last a lifetime. But too many people never do. I didn't know how it was for Chuck, being on the top level like he was, because he didn't tell me. It just isn't something you can tell that easy.

On the way home, Coach Rose said that if Chuck hadn't been in the race, I would have beat the state record myself by more than four seconds. I tried to think about that, but it was too much, so I just spent a long time looking at my medal.

After we got home, the news was all over town in just a few minutes. I was hoping it would be. My mom hugged me. My dad shook my hand. Mr. Garland called from the John Deere store and told me that he wouldn't make me work overtime to make up the day I missed, since I did so good. He was teasing, of course, but not as much as it sounded.

The next day in church, I wore my medal, but not so anybody could see. Chuck came and we sat together. During announcements Brother Bob had us stand up and he told the whole church what we had done. Everybody clapped. That surprised me, since we don't clap much in our church. When somebody does well in church, you are supposed to say, "Amen," loud enough for other people to hear. Amen is more religious than clapping. But they clapped for us. I guess that was because what we had done was not all that religious.

"Do the Right Thing"

That Monday morning, Chuck and I were called to Mr. Benalli's office during first hour. They didn't even wait until study hall, but called us right out of class. Mr. Benalli and Coach Rose seemed really happy. They both shook our hands and congratulated us, but Casteel didn't say a word. When we sat down, he stared straight at Chuck, and then said, "Did you run as fast as you could Saturday?" I didn't know why he was mad about it.

Chuck looked at him for a while, hooked one leg over the arm of his chair, crinkled his eyes and said, "Well, maybe not. I had a little left at the end."

"How much?" Casteel sounded even madder.

"That's hard to say," and Chuck started to say more, but Casteel interrupted.

"Twenty-one seconds more?"

"That's quite a lot." Chuck used the same tone he used with me when he told me my stories were funny.

"What do you mean a lot? Twenty-one seconds isn't any time at all. I can hold my breath that long." Casteel used the tone he used when he caught someone skipping school.

Chuck didn't say anything while he untied and retied his shoe.

But then he said, "It's nearly two seconds a lap, and that is quite a lot. Why do you ask?"

"Because," Mr. Casteel's neck was red, "you're going to run in the state meet a week from Saturday, and I want a national record. I want it for this school. I want it for this town. You owe that to me, to us. This is the biggest thing almost that ever happened to this town, and I want it—national publicity. We have fame too close to lose."

Chuck changed legs over the chair and he said, "I don't know. Maybe I could pick up two seconds a lap somewhere. But I don't know."

"What do you need?" Casteel asked like it was more of a threat than a question.

Chuck was quiet for a while like he was thinking. "It wouldn't hurt to have somebody run in front of me and set the pace and break the wind."

"Delbert can do that, can't he?" When Casteel said that, it almost surprised me. I was beginning to think he didn't know I was in the room. Now, even though he was talking to Chuck, he was at least talking about me.

"Well, he's fast enough." Chuck said it like he wasn't so sure.

"So what's the problem?" Casteel was in a bigger hurry than Chuck.

"What if he runs out of gas himself?" Chuck asked.

"Well, go around him," Casteel almost yelled. "Then you can finish on your own."

"But that's going to sacrifice his chances." Chuck was calm. "He could get beat for second place—or he might not even finish."

Casteel was calmer now, but he still acted like he was superintendent and we were only students. "That doesn't matter, as long as I get that record. Coach, I'm holding you personally responsible for this. You have done all right up to this point, but I want that record." He turned and walked out.

Coach Rose and Mr. Benalli sat and looked at each other for a long time. Chuck looked at them and I just looked at the floor.

Coach Rose said, "I'll walk you back to your rooms." I thought he would talk to us about running, but he didn't. He told us a story which didn't have anything to do with anything. He told us about some kid named Icarus who made himself wings so he could fly. But when he flew too close to the sun his wings melted. When we got to the door, he just said, "I'm going to expect you guys to do the right thing," and he walked off.

That afternoon, we ran ten miles slow. We wanted to work the aches out from the race, and also to get the breathing right for some serious running later on that week. Along the way, we both noticed things like the wheat growing and the trees up on the hill getting greener and the birds flying, and we even saw a garden snake wiggling across the road. We laughed a lot, tried to sing some, and talked about what it meant to win the district track meet.

When we were almost back to the Whippet and running smooth I said, "That sure is a goofy plan of Casteel's isn't it?"

Chuck said, "Is it?" like maybe he didn't know.

"Sure," I told him. "I can't run that fast that long. I would die before I got in."

"Yes," he said rather quiet, "but I sure would like to have that record."

When I looked over at him, his eyes weren't crinkled.

We didn't say anything the rest of the way in to the Whippet. When we got there, a lot of football players were waiting around to watch us come in and talk to us about racing. They brought both of us cherry limeades. Then a couple of them sat with Chuck on the tailgate of the old Chevy dangling their feet while I stood by myself, over by the cab.

29

"I Can Run Too!"

On Tuesday of that week, we ran half-mile sprints and jogged half-miles in between, so we didn't talk much. On Wednesday, when we ran out to the cemetery and back, we talked some, but it sounded almost like strangers instead of two guys who had been over the road as often as we had. I knew we were just killing time; we couldn't put off the issue forever. We both had done some thinking and now we had to talk about it. Two friends can't go through life not talking—it just isn't healthy.

So just as we started back to town, I asked, "How do you feel about it now?" He knew what I was talking about.

"Just as I did Monday." He wasn't mad, but I could tell he wasn't going to back down.

"I still don't know." I said the truth. "It seems like it is almost cheating."

"It isn't cheating," he said like he had been around enough to know. "That kind of thing is done all the time."

"But it seems like such a risk." I was trying to be reasonable.

"What's so risky?" He wanted to know.

"What if I can't run fast enough to set that pace?" I wasn't just being modest. I wanted to know.

"You can." He said it like he wasn't bragging on me.

"What if *you* can't run that fast?" I was just wondering.

After a while, he said, "I can," and it sounded the same way it did when he said it about me.

I still wasn't convinced. "What if this doesn't work? Then what?"

"It will," is all he said.

After a few steps, I said, kind of soft but so that he knew I meant it, "What if I am faster than you?"

"You aren't." He said it like he was still just telling facts.

"Care to prove that?" I know that sounded like a dare, but I think I meant for it to.

"Sure," he said, and we both took off running, faster even than we had run on Saturday. Although we were almost three miles out, I was determined to beat him. I set my pace up, pulled my long legs out as fast as I could, pumped my arms, and held my eyes straight down the road. I was ahead of him, but not by much. I thought I would run a little faster, but he stayed right with me. When I got to running about as fast as I could, I just held the pace, and he followed me.

I remember going by the first mile, and I remember running most of the second mile, but somewhere I kind of lost contact with the real world. My heart was beating so hard I could feel it, and my head began to hurt. If he hadn't been so close behind me, I would have slowed down, but I couldn't. I just couldn't let him catch up, so all I thought about was running. I could see the Whippet all right, and just focused my mind and body on that and kept running. After a while, I couldn't feel my legs, and thought I was floating on a cloud. But I knew I wasn't because everything hurt too bad—my legs and head, and my chest, and even my arms. I want to let them drop and relax them but I was afraid to. Chuck was too close for me to take a chance. I remember coming closer to the Whippet, knowing I was still ahead and working hard to stay that way. I heard Casteel's words and Chuck's words and I knew I was going to show them. I could run too. I just might set that old record.

I was ahead. That was all I knew, and all I needed to know. I had the willpower to beat him. The Whippet came closer and closer and finally I could see the old Chevy and I knew we were almost there. I could hold out. I had to. But right before we came to the edge of the Whippet, maybe fifty yards out, I saw something out of the corner of my eye. Chuck was by my side. I had to run faster; somehow I had to run faster. Even though I hurt, that thought had to carry me past the pain. I *had* to run faster. So we ran like that, side by side, for maybe another twenty-five yards. When I was running as fast as I could, Chuck pulled ahead and there was nothing I could do. Maybe if I just kept running, he would trip or slow down or fall in a pothole. But he didn't. By the time we came to the edge of the Whippet, he was far enough ahead that I could see all of his back, and we ran into the parking lot that way.

I couldn't see much, but I heard some people, and they were clapping. Somebody handed me a towel and I wiped the sweat off my face and out of my eyes before they could see it wasn't all sweat. After standing and walking around a bit, I got my sight back enough to see people, some football players, some girls from school and even a few grown-ups. I guess they had come down to see us run. Then I spotted him, over by the old Chevy, drooping over, head bent down, arms dangling. His legs wobbled as he stood.

I walked over to the Whippet window and bought a jumbo cherry limeade—but only one.

Breakfast at the Dew Drop

We continued to run every day that week and the next, but we never talked. We just went about our business, knowing what we had to do each day. I bought my cherry limeades and he bought his. At school we didn't talk in study hall. We still sat together at lunch, but now we were in the middle of the crowd—football players, girls, even cheerleaders—so we didn't have to say anything to each other.

He never came over to my house anymore. At church on Sunday, he sat beside me, and we even sang out of the same hymnbook, but we didn't talk.

Connie Faye and I went out a couple of times that week. Now, I know the experts say you aren't supposed to be around girls while you are in training, but I don't know why. We had gone out together before and that didn't seem to hurt me, so I couldn't see anything wrong with it now. Besides, she never talked about running, didn't mention it once; and she never talked about him either. I liked her for that.

Isn't life funny? At that district track meet, I stood on that second level with that medal around my neck and felt something I had never felt before, and now I didn't even want to talk about it. I couldn't understand how things had changed so fast.

At night, I would wake up and see pictures of myself beating him right at the line. I would drop off back to sleep and wake up again, this time seeing pictures of him beating me. Then I would wake up again and see myself standing way off somewhere watching him finish. I didn't know what to think.

Brother Bob had told us once that the Bible has the right answer to every question, so I tried that. Since I didn't know the Bible as well as I should, and didn't know where to look for help, I just dropped it open and started reading right there. The first time, I got a bunch of begats over in the Old Testament, and I knew that wouldn't help. The next time, it opened to the Song of Solomon, and I can't even tell you what that said. The third time, I got over in Matthew where it tells about Jesus going to a place named Gethsemane. He told the disciples to watch, but they kept going to sleep. But when he was by Himself, He prayed, "Not as I will." I wasn't sure I knew what all that meant, but it did give me something more to think about.

Sunday night after church, Mr. Garland called and asked if I could come to breakfast at the Dew Drop the next morning. I said, "Sure," and then lay awake wondering what he wanted to talk about. I thought I had been doing my job okay. I had asked for two Saturdays off, to go to the district track meet and then to the state, but I didn't think he was mad about that. If he had wanted to fire me, he wouldn't have invited me to the Dew Drop but would have told me right in the store.

When I got to breakfast, Mr. Garland was there, but so was half the town, and even some who didn't live in town—Moss Bosco, Earl Bresserman, Lyman Jones, lots of others—even Mr. Benalli, who didn't say anything except, "Hi."

Mr. Garland was very nice. He asked me to sit at his table and told me to order anything I wanted. I thought about ordering steak and eggs. I'd heard that rich people have steak and eggs for breakfast, and thought that just for one day I might eat what rich people do. But instead, I ordered bacon and eggs and listened to the conversation. They talked about how good the wheat was and how fat the cattle were and how long we could go before we needed rain again. They complained about the president and long-haired hippies and judges who turn people loose—the usual things.

Then it kind of got quiet, like something big was about to happen. Mr. Garland spoke to me loud enough for everybody to hear. "Delbert, let's talk about you. How's the running going?"

"Good, Sir." By then I was almost finished with my eggs but I still had a piece of toast and jelly I sort of wanted to eat.

"Well, that's good news." He said it like he was speaking for the whole group and maybe the whole town. "We just wanted to bring you down here to tell you how important this is to Wheatheart," and several said something like, "Sure is," or "Uh-huh," and things like that.

Mr. Jones said, "As big as a state championship football game, it seems to me."

"Maybe even bigger," Mr. Garland added. Then he said, "We thought about calling Chuck down, but we decided not to, since you're the one who'll have to do all the work."

I looked at him like I didn't know what he was talking about. He just went on like I wasn't looking at him. "You've got to get out there in front and hold that lead long enough for him to reach the record time." I was surprised that he knew all about that, but I shouldn't have been. In Wheatheart your business belongs to everybody. And by the way these men talked, this was more than just my business.

Then they went around the room saying more things like, "We're counting on you," and "You can do it," and "Best thing that could ever happen to this town," and *Sports Illustrated*," and "National record," and things like that. Except Mr. Benalli never said anything.

All the time I sat there trying to figure everything out. Mr. Garland was talking about loyalty, and yet he didn't tell *Time* magazine that he was from Wheatheart.

Even though they tried to make me feel like a grown-up, I knew I wasn't, because none of it made sense to me.

31

The Sacrificial Lamb

I was glad when that breakfast meeting was over, but I shouldn't have bothered, since school was worse, and not just that day but all week. Everybody, football players, cheerleaders, even teachers, came up to me and said, "I think it's wonderful what you're going to do for Chuck." One morning, when I went into study hall, Mrs. Bell said, "There's that dear boy we are going to offer as a sacrificial lamb." I didn't know what she meant, but that was all right. I didn't understand a lot of things she talked about.

Everybody at school who had reason to speak to me said about the same thing that week and some of them more than once—everybody except Connie Faye and Coach Rose and Mr. Benalli. I didn't bother telling anyone that I wasn't going to do it. I didn't know how I was going to get out of it, but I had to.

Thursday was the last day we ran and then only for four miles. We still weren't speaking, but that was all right, since it gave me a chance to look at the wheat and hills going out and the town coming back. By then, the spring wheat had begun to put on heads of grain and all that growth now had purpose to it. You could see what it was for. The town was more beautiful than I had ever remembered it being. The trees and grass had greened up and the elevators looked so white standing next to all that green. Even if we weren't talking, I was still glad to be out running. When we were about a mile out, Chuck spoke and it sounded like the tone my sister used when my mother made her apologize for breaking the string on my guitar. "You can't do it."

"What?" I was a little surprised, but I also didn't want him to know I was thinking about it.

"You can't pace me Saturday." He said it in the same tone.

"Who said I was going to?" I snapped at him.

"You can't." He was still soft.

"Why not? You said yourself I was fast enough." I might have been a little snippy.

I waited a long time for him to speak and when he did it sounded like he didn't want to say it at all. "But what if *I'm* not?"

We didn't talk anymore after that. We just ran along, and I thought my thoughts and he thought his. I didn't know how he was doing with his thoughts, but I needed some help with mine. But I wasn't going to admit it, not then.

Friday was a big day in Wheatheart. During last hour, we were all called into the gym for an assembly. I thought it might be one of those traveling things where somebody rides a bicycle with only one wheel or two foreigners play Ping-Pong standing way back from the table. But it wasn't. It was a serious pep assembly for just me and Chuck. Some of the downtown people were there, Doc's receptionist and Mr. Garland and people like that. But I knew it was really serious because Mr. Casteel ran it himself. He had us sing the "Star-Spangled Banner" and the school fight song, and then he told them about the race over at Alva like he had been there. He said that Chuck had a chance at the national record. He didn't say anything about me. He just told them about him. Then he gave us each a box. We stood there in front of everybody and opened them. I don't like to get gifts, and I especially don't like to get them in front of a crowd like that. I am sure my face turned red. Inside the boxes were brand new running suits, green with white stripes all across. We thanked Mr. Casteel, and the assembly was over.

Since Mr. Garland had given me the day off and I wasn't supposed to run, I had the rest of the afternoon to myself; so I got out the old 12-gauge and drove up to the hills along the river. This time, I didn't even take a shell. The hills were really green from a distance and even greener when I got inside them.

For a long time, I just stood there and looked down toward town, across eight miles of wheat fields. That time of year, eight miles of wheat fields is a sight worth looking at. All that wheat was so green and looked so rich—like money in the bank. But it wasn't fully grown. And a lot of things could happen between now and harvest. In the spring when the wheat looks rich and thick, like it was now, farmers can begin to plan what they might buy new, but they can't make the down payment until after the harvest.

I just walked and walked, trying to decide what I was going to do. For some people it might not have been much of a decision, but for me it was. The worst part of it was that I was so lonely, so by myself. Oh, a lot of people had offered to help me, all right, to tell me what I ought to do. But they were telling me what *they* wanted me to do for *them*. And they weren't the ones taking a risk. I was.

I knew I wasn't as fast as Chuck. We had proved that. I could have said that I slipped or something at the last. In fact, I wanted to say that, but it wasn't true. He had outrun me; but even then, I liked being in second place. Oh, I know we are all supposed to want to be in first place, but I had never been as high as second place until that day at Alva and I liked being there. There isn't anything wrong with being second, and I could be second place at the state meet. I knew I could. Coach Rose had told me that I outran the record by four seconds.

But if I paced Chuck, I would be a part of a national record and no one would even remember my name or my part in it. Nobody but me.

Then I thought of Chuck, wondering how he would feel with a national record. I guessed he would feel pretty good. But how would he feel if I paced him and dropped out, and he didn't get the record? I thought about that for a long time, and I sighed some.

If this pacing were a sure thing, it might be different. I could live with knowing I had a part in it. But nobody could guarantee it, not Casteel or the men at the Dew Drop or Coach Rose. If it didn't work, I would have lost seocnd place for nothing.

Then I remembered something Mrs. Bell had said about my being a sacrifice. That wheat seed the farmers stuck in the ground last fall was a sacrifice, what with the bugs and dry weather and hail out to get it. I looked out across the eight miles of wheat fields and realized how those sacrifices paid off. But then I thought, "If I do this it will be because I want to, not because I have to. Is it a sacrifice if you want to?" As I drove home, I remembered what Christ had said to His Father, just before He became a sacrifice—"Not as I will." But I still didn't know if I wanted to pace him or finish second.

About nine o'clock that night I was in my room thinking about going to bed and trying to get some sleep for the big day, when my mom knocked. I was glad she did. In fact, I wanted her to come in and tell me what to do. She and I had talked about it—talked a lot. I had helped her wash dishes more during the last week than all my time growing up. She did help me think through things—like about Casteel and Mr. Garland; but when I asked her what I should do, she would only say, "I am proud of you, no matter what you do, you know that." Well, of course that helped, but I still wanted her to tell me what I should do.

But that night when she came to my room, she didn't have any new advice. She told me I had a visitor. I thought of a hundred people it could have been, and one I hoped it was, when Coach Rose walked right into my room. He didn't even look uncomfortable and he didn't glance around like he was criticizing. He just scooted some underwear and socks off the side of the bed and sat down and looked like he was resting. He was friendly, but he didn't waste much time telling me what he had to say.

"Delbert, let me tell you something about tomorrow. You are going to run a race. Don't make it anything bigger than that. One problem with sports is that people try to make them the most important thing and put all their hopes and happiness on the outcome, and that's silly. Regardless of what happens tomorrow, regardless of whether Chuck sets the national record or even finishes, there are still going to be hungry people in the world and crime in the City. Make up your mind about what you have to do. Remember, regardless of what anybody had said to you, it's your decision. Just do your best. But above all, have a good time, because that's what footraces and football games are for. That is all they are for, for people to have a good time. Now get some sleep." He walked out and I slept better than I had for at least two weeks.

Discovering the Reason

The stadium was crowded by the time we got there the next day. And more of the crowd than I had ever expected was from Wheatheart. They had turned out almost like they do for the state championship football games.

The state track meet was even more of a circus than the district had been; I wasn't sure I was ready for that. After we had put our new suits on and wandered out onto the field, I thought we would spend the rest of the time just lying around and resting like we had before; but this was harder. For one thing, everybody knew who Chuck was, and they all came up and talked to him like he was some kind of a big deal. Then the people from Wheatheart kept coming around. I don't know how they managed to get onto the middle of the field, with the policemen trying to keep them off, but they did. Connie Faye and Darla Sue came and took pictures. Mr. Casteel was there to yell at us. I don't think he meant to sound that way, but he did. Coach Rose was there, of course; it was his job, but he made it seem like more than that.

I hadn't figured on so much company. I thought I would have time to get off by myself during the day and make some decisions—I still didn't know yet how I was going to run. I knew Coach Rose hadn't meant to confuse me, but he had. I just didn't know what to do. When I saw the big crowd, I knew it would be nice to stand on that second level and have somebody put a medal around my neck.

With all the confusion, I was actually glad when the man with the loudspeaker said, "First call for the 5,000 meter." I was glad the time had come, but I wished I knew what I was going to do. We lined up on the track, stretched, and limbered up. One official was saying things like "Twelve laps around and finish at the other end," things we already knew. The official with the gun was putting shells in it. Everybody was trying to act friendly and relaxed, but nobody was. Some of the runners were trying to crowd in around Chuck, shake his hand and wish him well, things like that. But he broke away from them and came over to me. He held out his hand and I took it. Then he said, "Run for yourself today, Osgood. Just run for yourself and no one else."

"I intend to." And then I said, but I don't know why, "If you run beside me, I'll tell you a story." He just crinkled his eyes, and the man with the gun moved on the track. We all crowded up to the front, he shot, and we started running. I couldn't see Chuck in the middle of the bunch, but I knew he was there. I got caught in the back again and had to run that way around the first curve, but then I moved over in the other lane and started passing people. About halfway down, I came up side by side by Chuck. We ran that way for a while. He was just running and looking straight ahead, but he knew I was there. I could tell that we were the fastest two in the race, though not by as much as the last time.

I knew I could just fall in behind him, follow him the rest of the way and pick up that second place. Or, I could get ahead of him and help him run for the record.

I would like to tell you I thought about all the good times we had together and all we had been through. But I didn't. I would like to tell you I thought about what everybody had said all week, but I didn't. I would like to tell you I thought about Christ saying, "Not as I will," but I didn't. I didn't think of any of those things. I just thought of standing on that box and getting that medal.

But while I was thinking about that, I speeded up and passed Chuck. When I got to the front, I set the pace as fast or maybe a little faster than I had run the day on Cemetery Road. When we got back around to where we had started, some man was counting: 65, 66, 67, 68; I guess if I had stopped to figure it out, I would have known we were on the right pace. But I didn't have time for that. I just knew I was running about as fast as I could. I didn't know what I was going to do when I got tired, but I would worry about that later. Right then, I was happy just running. I didn't know how far back Chuck was, but I thought I could feel him right behind me.

I tried looking around some, but people in a crowd aren't as pretty as spring wheat; and besides, I didn't want to waste the time. So I just looked straight ahead and made my own pictures in my mind. We ran that way, lap after lap. I knew I was going to get tired, but I wasn't sure when. My head was already beginning to hurt and my chest was really pounding. But we just kept running. Most of the time I was so busy I didn't even notice the cards telling us how many laps we had left. But I did see the one that said 3 and I thought for a minute that I might just be able to run that way another three laps and win myself; but rather than doing that, I speeded up even more. That was too much for me. My eyes were so bleary I was just running by feel. I couldn't even see the track, much less the crowd, or even the other runners, but I kept running. I don't know how far I ran that way. I couldn't tell much of anything, except that I was running. My mind wandered off so that I didn't think of anything. I just kept running.

But somewhere, sometime, I felt my left leg blow out. It just went limp like I couldn't tell it what to do anymore. I stepped toward my left to keep my balance and could tell I was running but I wasn't on the track anymore. I first thought I had to get back on the track some way, but then it didn't matter, and soon I wasn't running at all anymore. I thought about falling down, but somebody caught me and we walked together. When my head cleared some, I looked at the other person. It was Coach Rose. He smiled at me and said, "Now I have two heroes." I could tell the race was still going on, but for a moment I forgot why. I was more miserable than I had ever been in my whole life, but I felt good too. Isn't that funny?

I saw a big crowd rush over to where we were supposed to finish, but I was still too hazy and too far away to know what was going on. The man on the loudspeaker was talking . . . somewhere in the middle he said, "National record," and I heard the crowd yell. I turned and looked at Coach Rose who still had his arm around my shoulders. He just looked at me and squeezed me with his arm, and we walked some more. Then I saw somebody walking toward us. Actually, he was staggering more than walking. His shoulders hung down low like he had been scooping seed wheat all day. His arms dangled like maybe his hands were too heavy for his body, and he bent over but tried to hold his head up like he had a sore back but he didn't want anybody to know. It was Chuck. I could tell that he was looking hard at me and that his eyes weren't crinkled.

When we got close enough, we both broke free from those holding us up and grabbed each other and held each other up. But we didn't do a very good job because we were both pretty wobbly. At first we laughed a bit, but it wasn't very loud. Then I think I cried some, but I don't know for sure about him.

Then he said so quiet nobody could hear, and so serious that I knew his eyes weren't crinkled, "Why, Osgood? Why did you do it?"

I didn't answer right away, for his "Why?" kept running through my hazy thoughts and hurting muscles. I remembered the first day Chuck and I met, when he asked me if I ever ran. That day I answered, "You mean, just run for no reason at all?" Like I told him, in Wheatheart we don't do things for no reason.

Well, today I had run with a reason, and I liked it that way. Somewhere, deep inside of me, I had chosen to do this and I knew the reason. It was as clear as I had ever known anything. But I wasn't sure I could ever explain it to anybody, not even to myself.

In the weeks since then, I've had time to go over the reason myself. I hadn't done it for Wheatheart. I knew that. Oh, I know those guys who tried to talk me into it, Mr. Garland, and all of them, are nice enough people and they don't mean any harm in thinking like they do. But they're wrong. They just want some glory.

But I knew, as I stood there in the middle of that football field in front of all those people, trying my best to hold up my wobbly-kneed friend, and I know now, that glory isn't worth a whole lot—not even the kind of glory that gets you talked about in John Deere conversations for years to come. That kind of glory is only who you are in the eyes of other people, and not really worth much at night after you turn the lights out and try to go to sleep.

And I hadn't done it for Chuck either-not really. Sure, he's my friend who needed me, but that makes it sound like I was just paying a debt, a debt to friendship.

Friendship is worth making some sacrifices for, but it can never be a debt or it wouldn't be friendship. I learned a lot from Chuck when we ran together in the spring and watched the wheat grow and turn into what it was meant to be. He taught me how to run hard and how to ask a girl out and how to look at wheat when it grows. But I taught him too, so I really didn't owe him anything.

I did it for another reason—for why Coach Rose is still at Wheatheart and for why my mom seems to be happy just being my mom and for why I couldn't forget Jimmy Charles after it seemed like everybody else in town had. That day of the race, for the first time in my life, somewhere about the third lap around the track, I suddenly knew that there is just something that is right, that always was right and always will be right, whether anybody else does it or not. And right is a good enough reason for doing something, even if you can't explain it.

Chuck leaned in closer and asked again, as serious as he was before, "Why did you do it, Osgood?"

I couldn't tell him the real reason, not then anyway. And so I just grinned at him and said, "What do you mean? I was trying to beat you. I didn't want to buy the cherry limeades."

I saw his eyes crinkle again as he said, "You're all right, Osgood. You're all right!"

I liked him better than I had ever liked him before.

Fiction From Victor Books

George MacDonald

A Quiet Neighborhood
The Seaboard Parish
The Vicar's Daughter
The Shopkeeper's Daughter
The Last Castle
The Prodigal Apprentice

Cliff Schimmels

Winter Hunger
Rivals of Spring
Summer Winds
Rites of Autumn

Robert Wise

The Pastors' Barracks

Donna Fletcher Crow

Brandley's Search
To Be Worthy